USA TODAY Bestselling Author

REBECCA YORK

Ruth Glick writing as Rebecca York

CARRIE'S PROTECTOR

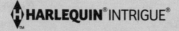

For two little eagles, E12 and E14,
who met untimely deaths in Decorah, Iowa.

Recycling programs
for this product may
not exist in your area.

ISBN-13: 978-0-373-74756-6

CARRIE'S PROTECTOR

Printed in U.S.A.

The moment their lips met, the kiss turned so hot that it could have started a wildfire.

The morning's adventure had driven both of them to the edge of desperation.

What she needed was to close her eyes and focus on the man who held her in his arms instead of everything else that was happening to her.

He deepened the kiss. She loved the taste of him, the feel of his body, the way he clasped her tightly. She'd been craving this since last night, and the terror of the past few hours had only intensified her emotions.

She forgot where they were, forgot everything except the need to get close to him—as close as two people could get.

ABOUT THE AUTHOR

Award-winning, *USA TODAY* bestselling novelist Ruth Glick, who writes as Rebecca York, is the author of more than one hundred books, including her popular 43 Light Street series for Harlequin Intrigue. Ruth says she has the best job in the world. Not only does she get paid for telling stories, she's also an author of twelve cookbooks. Ruth and her husband, Norman, travel frequently, researching locales for her novels and searching out new dishes for her cookbooks.

Books by Rebecca York

HARLEQUIN INTRIGUE

*43 Light Street
**Mindbenders

CAST OF CHARACTERS

Carrie Mitchell—Her troubles started when she overheard terrorists plotting to blow up a major D.C. landmark.

Wyatt Hawk—Assigned to protect Carrie and determined not to let their relationship get personal.

Douglas Mitchell—Carrie's father. Did he pick the wrong man to protect his daughter?

Bobby Thompson—The only terrorist the cops captured. What about the rest of them?

Skip Gunderson—Federal prosecutor who was supposed to get information from Carrie.

Harry, Sidney, Jordan and Bruce—The terrorists determined to save their friend from a prison term by getting rid of Carrie.

Patrick Harrison—Douglas Mitchell's chief of staff and a longtime friend of the family.

Quincy Sumner—He had a public fight with Douglas Mitchell over a land deal.

Aaron Madison—Did the federal prosecutor turn in Carrie for money?

Rita Madison—Aaron's estranged wife. Is she really a grieving widow?

Chapter One

Carrie Mitchell had made the biggest mistake of her life. And if she had it to do all over again, her actions would be exactly the same.

"Ready?" the dark-haired man waiting ramrod straight at the bottom of the stairs asked.

She dragged in a breath and let it out before speaking. "As ready as I'm going to be."

"Then let's get it over with."

He stepped outside and motioned for her to wait as he looked around the exterior of the safe house where she'd been staying for the past week.

Really, the visual inspection was unnecessary, she thought. Nobody could get past the electric fence and the motion detectors, or through the main gate without the proper security codes.

Still, he made her linger inside before motioning her out the door, then led the way toward the black town car they were taking into D.C. The car was bulletproof, a precaution Carrie wished they could have done without. But her father, Douglas Mitchell, was rich enough to make his own rules when it came to his daughter's safety—or anything else. An ordinary man would have relied on the FBI to protect his only child. Dad wanted an armored car and an elite private security team to keep her safe. The driver was already behind the wheel, a guy named Joe Collins, who was one of the guards who had been with her for the past week.

The man who held the car door open was Wyatt Hawk, the one in charge. Carrie didn't like him much. Maybe that wasn't fair, because she couldn't really say she knew him. He kept himself so closed up that she'd had little chance for an in-depth conversation with him.

He was tall and muscular and good-looking in a kind of tough-guy way that she might have admired from a distance—if she'd had the choice. You could imagine him as the bodyguard for a mob boss, although that wasn't his background. He was supposed to have retired early from the CIA, but he never talked about his former life.

The other security men at the safe house were much more open about their backgrounds. They were all ex-cops, and they'd been friendly, perhaps to counteract Wyatt's aloof demeanor. Gary Blain was a black man in his fifties, with a shaved head and broad shoulders. Hank Swinton was around the same age, with a bit of gray invading his sandy hair. And Rodrigo Garcia was a little younger, with classic Hispanic features.

They'd made her feel protected as they'd tried to

lighten her isolation. In contrast, Wyatt always had an open book in front of him at the dining table, probably to discourage conversation. One of the few things she knew about him was that he liked World War II spy novels.

She'd joined him a time or two in the basement gym. He'd stuck to his routine of weight machines and hard-driving pumping on the elliptical trainer to the sounds of classic rock.

She never pushed herself as far. For her, exercise wasn't a religion. It was just a way to keep in reasonable shape so she could crawl around in the woods taking pictures of wildlife.

Which was how she'd gotten into the worst trouble of her life.

Last Thursday she'd been practicing her profession, happily eavesdropping on an eagles' nest in D.C.'s Rock Creek Park, the sprawling wooded area that ran through the northwest section of the city. She'd been using her telephoto lens to capture the family life of the parents and their two babies, photographing them off and on since before they'd hatched.

The photos were to illustrate a piece she was doing for *Wildlife Magazine* on raptors in urban areas.

She was creeping through the underbrush out of sight of the eagles' eighty-foot-high, thousand-pound nest when she spotted three young Midwestern-looking men in jeans and T-shirts in a nearby picnic area.

She could see they hadn't come for a meal. They

were sitting at one of the tree-shaded wooden tables, speaking in low voices. Two of them were chain-smoking and littering the ground with the spent butts. Every so often, one of them would look around nervously.

At first she'd paid them only minimal attention. Then, as she moved to get a different angle on the nest, she started to get the gist of their conversation, and the back of her neck began to tingle.

She heard the words *bomb, Capitol Police* and *best place to inflict maximum damage*. Her heart was pounding as she swiveled cautiously in her hidden position, switching her camera's focus from the eagles' nest to the men. After taking their pictures, she wanted to flee, yet she knew that just their faces might not be enough to identify them. Her every move stealthy, she made her way back toward the road, intent on getting their license plates, as well. Her own car was parked on the other side of the picnic area, because it was a better approach to the eagles' nest.

Finally she was on the verge of pressing her luck too far. The men were still talking as she circled back the way she'd come, knowing she'd better get out of the woods before they spotted her.

But she realized it was already too late when she heard a shout of alarm.

"Hey, somebody's spying on us."

Her heart in her throat, she started running flat

out for her car, hearing the crack of twigs and the rustle of underbrush behind her. She fumbled in her bag for the car remote, clicking the lock as she pelted through the woods.

She was only seconds ahead of them as she jumped into the driver's seat and started the engine. As she pulled away, she heard the sound of gunfire.

The back window and a taillight shattered as she sped away. But she made it onto Military Road and out of the park, and they didn't pick up her trail because they'd had to double back and circle around to get to the other parking area. She'd made it to the nearest police station, and the rest was history.

Her attention snapped back to the present when Wyatt spoke.

"You okay?" he asked.

"Yes."

"The Federal prosecutor has the pictures you took of the men. All you have to do is tell him exactly what you heard and exactly what happened."

"Then I suppose I'll have to show up in court for Bobby Thompson's trial." He was the only one of the men who had been identified and arrested. He was locked up in a maximum-security facility while the others were still at large.

"Not for months."

"Does that mean we're going to be together for months?" she asked, sorry she couldn't keep the snappish tone out of her voice.

"NOT NECESSARILY," WYATT answered. Not if he could help it. He wanted out of this situation, but not until he got a suitable replacement.

He slid Carrie a sidewise glance, noting the way she was twisting her fingers together in her lap. He wanted to reach over and press his hand over hers, but he kept his arms at his sides because he knew that touching her was a bad idea.

His gaze traveled to her short-cropped dark hair. When they'd first met, it had been long and blond, but he'd made her cut and dye it—to change her appearance. She hadn't liked it, but she'd done it—then refused contact lenses that would change her blue eyes to brown. And there was no way to disguise her high cheekbones, cute little nose or appealing lips. She was still a very attractive woman, even with the change in her hair and the nondescript clothing he'd purchased for her. As they rode into town, she looked like a Federal employee who'd come in on a Saturday to catch up on her work.

They made the rest of the trip into the District in silence, a silence he'd tried to maintain since he'd first met her. She probably thought he didn't like her. The problem was just the opposite. He liked her a lot. She had courage and determination, and she wasn't like a lot of rich women who thought that the world owed them special consideration. She was hardworking, smart and good at her job. She had all the qualities he admired in a woman, which was why he couldn't allow himself to get close to her.

To his relief, the long ride was almost over. At least they wouldn't be confined to the backseat of a car for much longer. While she talked with the prosecutor, he could wait in the reception area.

"The building's just ahead," he said in a low voice, breaking the silence inside the sedan.

Beside him Carrie sighed. "I guess the sooner I get this over with, the sooner I get my life back."

"Makes sense," he answered, wondering if she ever would get her life back. Would she ever feel safe again tramping around in the woods by herself, photographing the subjects she loved to capture in their natural environment? For just a moment he pictured himself going on those expeditions with her, carrying her equipment, making sure that nobody got out of line with her and no wild animals attacked her. Then he ruthlessly cut off that avenue of thought before it could go any further. He and Carrie Mitchell were from two different worlds. She had had every advantage growing up. She could have lived off her dad for the rest of her life, but she was trying to make a name for herself in a difficult profession. He was an ex-spook who came from a family in Alexandria, Virginia, that was barely making it. His dad drove a cab. His mom was a waitress, and he'd known he wanted a different life, which was why he'd joined the army and then the CIA. He'd seen a lot of the world, but he was home now and working private security. And even if their backgrounds matched better, he was too damaged to even think about a relationship with someone like her—or any-one else, for that matter.

They were meeting Skip Gunderson, the Federal prosecutor, in a yellow-brick government building as nondescript as Carrie's clothing. Five stories tall, with a security barrier at the entrance. As a precau-tion, it wasn't the building where Gunderson nor-mally worked. The meeting was at another facility that was off the radar of the D.C. press corps.

That was one of the unfortunate aspects of this whole situation. Although Carrie's identity was sup-posed to be confidential, somehow a cable news reporter had gotten wind of her name. Now every-one and his brother knew that she was the woman who had foiled a major terrorist plot. At least they hadn't been able to ferret out the location of the safe house where she was staying. Or photograph her dis-guise—he hoped.

"Showtime," Carrie murmured, as the big car made a right turn and pulled up at the metal stan-chions that blocked the entrance to an underground garage. Next to the barrier was a guardhouse, where a man in a blue uniform and police-type cap stood as if he had an iron pipe rammed up his butt. Wyatt watched him. Usually these guys were relaxed, but the guard's posture pegged him as being on edge.

As their car stopped, he stepped out.

Wyatt hadn't seen him before, but then, he hadn't seen a lot of the men assigned to security duty at this place.

"Identification, please," the guard said to Joe Collins, the driver, who rolled down his window and reached into his pocket for the papers.

Wyatt had heard the request every time they'd arrived here, yet today something was just a bit off—perhaps the hint of edginess in the man's voice or the way he had his cap pulled down low. That thought had barely crossed Wyatt's mind when the man raised his arm, aiming an automatic pistol toward the open window of the car.

Acting on instinct and experience, Wyatt pushed Carrie down, blocking her body with his as he pulled out his own weapon and wrenched himself around to face the guard.

He was a split second too late to prevent disaster.

Joe went down in a spray of blood. Wyatt fired at the bogus guard, striking him in the chest and knocking him backward into the glass booth. But undoubtedly, he wasn't the only threat. Before the man hit the ground, Wyatt lunged across the car and opened the opposite door, pushing Carrie out ahead of him.

She gasped as she came down on the hard cement of the driveway.

"Sorry. We've got to get the hell out of here, but not onto the street."

Looking up, he confirmed that assessment as he saw eight armed men racing down the driveway toward them—men who didn't look like cops or security guards.

Carrie followed his gaze, gasping as she took in the situation.

Grabbing her hand, he helped her up, leading her toward the right and behind a row of cars in the garage, giving them some cover. But he was badly outnumbered and outgunned. He wasn't going to shoot it out with these guys in the garage if he could help it.

"This way."

He'd studied the layout of the building, and he hurried her along the wall and around a corner to a service door and was relieved to find it unlocked.

"We have to call the police," she whispered when the door closed behind them.

"No. We can't trust the police or anyone else. *Somebody* gave up the meeting."

As he spoke, he considered their options. Going down would trap them in the lower floors of the garage. Which left only one alternative.

"We're going up."

They had just reached the third level when Wyatt heard gunfire blasting below.

He led Carrie through a door into the building, then pulled out his cell phone and speed-dialed the safe house.

Gary Blain answered. "Wyatt? Is something wrong?"

"Yeah. We're in the building where Carrie was supposed to meet the prosecutor. Somehow the terrorists knew we were coming."

"Is she all right?"

"Yes. But there are shooters in here."

"Where are you?"

"Near the south stairwell. Armed men were blocking the garage entrance. Can you pick us up on the roof?"

"Negative. Unless we get clearance for a helo flight into D.C."

Wyatt answered with a curse.

A burst of gunfire from below interrupted the conversation.

"Gotta go."

He led Carrie down the hall to another stairwell then up two more levels. He was pretty sure the attackers had thought they'd get him and Carrie in the garage, which meant they probably hadn't stationed anyone up here. Yet.

Cautiously he opened the door and looked out into the hallway. Nothing was moving—particularly the dead body lying in a pool of blood in the center of the tile floor.

When he hesitated, Carrie pressed against his back and looked over his shoulder.

"Oh, God," she breathed as she gazed at Skip Gunderson, the Federal prosecutor she'd been coming to meet.

"We can't stay here," Wyatt said.

But when he glanced back at Carrie, he saw the blood had drained from her face and she had gone stock-still.

"Carrie!"

Her gaze stayed on Gunderson. "We have to…" she whispered.

He gripped her arm, squeezing hard. "I'm sorry, but there's nothing you can do for him now."

When she still didn't move, he tugged on her arm. "Come on. Before we end up the same way."

He watched her expression harden as she shook herself into action and let him lead her down the hall, although she kept looking back.

"This is my fault," she said, as he tried to determine the best place to hide.

"You're not responsible."

She made a snorting sound. "Of course I am. He was here to meet me."

"Because he was doing his job. Maybe you should blame the building security for letting terrorists in here. Or whoever leaked the meeting information."

He hurried Carrie down the hall, opening doors as they went. Most led to small offices, but one was larger, which had the potential for more hiding places. He stepped inside, looking around. The blinds were partially closed, which would give them more cover. Crouching behind the broad wooden desk was too obvious, but a bank of storage cabinets blocked the view from the door.

"Get back there."

"What about you?"

"I'm coming."

Carrie hesitated, then crossed the room and wedged

herself into the corner. Crossing to the desk, he opened drawers, looking for anything useful. When he found a box of pushpins, he threw them onto the polished tile floor, watching them scatter. Then he crossed to the cabinets and stepped in front of Carrie, gun drawn.

Of course, if he had to shoot, he'd alert every terrorist in the building.

As he pressed his back to her front, he could feel the tension humming through her.

"Wyatt?"

"I'm here to make sure you get out of this." He wanted to turn around and take her in his arms. He wanted to stroke her back and hair to comfort her, but he knew that facing the enemy was more important than giving her reassurances.

Down the hall, Wyatt could hear rapid footsteps and doors opening and slamming shut again. When the door to the office where they were hiding opened, every muscle in his body tensed. He saw a shadow flicker on the wall—the shadow of a man holding a machine gun. The guy stood still for a moment, then started across the tile floor toward their hiding place.

Chapter Two

Wyatt waited, his body coiled for action.

In a couple of seconds, if the trap he'd set didn't work, the invader was going to spot them—and shoot. But before he reached their hiding place, the man stepped on the pushpins and lost his footing.

Wyatt sprang around the corner, reaching for the guy's gun arm and pulling him forward across the slippery surface. Off balance from the pins and the man yanking on his arm, the gunman scrambled to stay upright while he tried to get his weapon into firing position. Before he could do either, Wyatt kicked him square in the back, sending him sprawling on the tile floor, yelping as the sharp points of the pins dug into his hands and face.

He was a blond guy, young and muscular, and totally unprepared to be attacked by the quarry he was hunting.

Wyatt was on him as he went down. As the guy struggled to respond to the changed circumstances, Wyatt raised his own weapon and bashed the terrorist over the head with the gun butt. The man went still.

"Cover him," he told Carrie, handing her his Sig while he looked for something to tie the guy up.

She held the weapon in a two-handed grip. He noted that she was savvy enough to stand a couple of yards away so that the man couldn't grab her leg if he came to and went into attack mode.

Wyatt's glance raked the desk. Grabbing the phone, he yanked the cord from the wall, then disconnected the cord from the phone to the receiver.

While Carrie kept the gun trained on the guy, Wyatt tied him up using both cords. When he was finished, he took a closer look at the terrorist's appearance. Definitely not from the Middle East. In fact, he looked like a typical Midwestern farmer with sunburned skin, blond hair and pleasant-enough features.

"You know him?" Wyatt asked. "Was he one of the men in the park?"

"No," Carrie answered.

"Well, that's a clue to the scope of the organization. Looks like the initial three you spotted in the park weren't the only ones involved in the plot."

She nodded.

As Blondie started to stir, Wyatt took back the gun while he debated what to do.

The man's eyes blinked open. When he tried to move and found that his hands and feet were secured, he swung his murderous gaze from Wyatt to Carrie and back again. Carrie recoiled, but Wyatt ignored the threatening scowl. "How many men are in the building?"

"Enough to kill you and the bitch."

"I don't think so." He wanted to ask how the terrorists had discovered the time and location of Carrie's meeting with the Federal prosecutor, but he knew that would only be a waste of time.

The guy smirked at him. "You won't get out of here alive. And once you're dead, there won't be anyone to testify against Bobby."

"They have the pictures she took of your meeting."

"So what? In this day and age, they could be faked. And—"

To stave off another smart remark, Wyatt bashed him on the head again, and he went still.

Carrie made a low, distressed sound. "Why did you do that?"

"Don't tell me you wanted to keep listening to his line of crap?"

"No."

Wyatt found packing tape in one of the desk drawers, and wound it around the guy's head and over his mouth so he couldn't call for help. Then he pulled him behind the desk.

"It looked like you handled my gun all right," he remarked.

"Yes. My father made sure I was able to protect myself."

"Good."

He handed her his automatic and took the terrorist's weapon for himself before crossing to the door and looking out. The hall was clear. But they'd come back when they realized their buddy was missing.

Wyatt led the way, and they sprinted to the end of the hall and into another office.

He locked the door, even knowing it would be a dead giveaway to their position. At least it would buy them a few seconds if somebody tried to get in.

"Up here the windows open. We can get out," he told Carrie.

"Five stories up?"

"There are step-back roofs." He hurried to the window and slid the glass open.

Carrie looked out, seeing the roof below them. "It's pretty far."

"Not if you lower yourself by your hands. I'll go first."

She kept her gaze on him. "You're all business. All the time. I should be thankful for that."

He bit back a retort. There was no time for anything but escape from a building that had turned into a death trap.

He slung the weapon over his shoulder, then climbed out the window and lowered himself, thankful that he was in good shape.

Controlling his descent, he eased down the wall, then let himself drop the four feet to the gravel surface of the roof below. Turning, he held up his arms to Carrie.

She shook her head. "I can't do that."

"You don't have to. I'll catch you. Hurry, before they find us."

She stuffed the gun into her shoulder bag, which she wrapped across her chest, then maneuvered herself out the window. Turning around, she lowered herself until her body was dangling from the frame. But her grip wasn't strong enough, and she fell. Wyatt was there to catch her, taking her weight as she came hurtling down.

They both wavered on their feet, then he steadied them.

"Thanks," she said.

"We've got to do that again."

She made a strangled sound but followed him to the edge of the roof. Again he went first, lowering himself to his full length, then dropping six feet to the roof below.

When he turned and glanced up, he saw Carrie watching him. She looked as if she wanted to protest; instead, she grimly climbed over the edge and lowered herself by her arms. This time she must have made a concerted effort to control her descent. She didn't let go until her full length was dangling from the edge. Again he caught her and staggered back, almost losing his balance. But he stayed on his feet, then went to check the next drop-off point.

A scuffling sound made him whirl around. He saw that Carrie had turned and was holding the pistol he'd given her in two hands—pointed at a man who was looking over the edge of the roof above, his weapon aimed downward.

Carrie fired, hitting the would-be assassin in the arm. Before he could recover, Wyatt delivered a chest shot, and the man went down, toppling over the edge and landing on the gravel surface a few yards from where they stood.

Carrie gasped as she stared at the body.

Wyatt hurried back to her, catching her look of horror as she realized what she'd done.

"I…I think he couldn't believe a woman had the guts to fire at him."

"His mistake," Wyatt said in a gritty voice. "Thank God you did."

She stood rigidly, and he reached for her hand.

"Gotta go."

At his touch, she shook herself into action, and he hustled her to the edge of the roof. This time there was a bonus feature: a ladder leading down to ground level.

Wyatt sent Carrie down first, alternately covering her descent and checking for more pursuers on the roof above. When he joined her, she was shaking, and he knew she was still reacting to what had happened.

"I shot a man," she whispered as though she were just now taking it in.

He pulled her toward him, at the same time easing her against the side of the building where it would be harder for anyone looking down from above to see them. Wrapping his arms around her, he held her close. "You shot in self-defense. He was going to kill you."

"It's not like shooting at a target."

He didn't point out that he'd fired the kill shot. Or that he'd killed a lot more men. This was no time for a philosophical discussion on the morality of protecting oneself.

She let her head drop to his shoulder, clinging to him, and he cradled her against himself, breathing in her scent, absorbing the curves of her slender body before easing away.

"We can't stay here. Another one of them could come across the roof at any minute. And there's a big clue up there about which way we went."

She shuddered, then looked around. "Why didn't we see any cops?"

"They may not know about it yet."

While he'd been holding her, he'd been thinking about escape routes. Before coming down to the government building with her today, he'd scouted out the area around the building as well as the interior, and he was mentally plotting a route that would get them onto the city streets.

He looked up one more time, scanning the roofline for terrorists before leading Carrie away from the building, toward a chain-link fence topped with barbed wire. He was wondering how they were going to get over it when he saw that the lock on the gate was broken and the barrier was open a crack.

"This must be how they were going to get away," he muttered as he pushed the gate farther open.

She nodded, following him through and into an alley.

He looked at the assault rifle in his hand. "I guess I can't take this out onto the street." First he used his shirt to wipe off his fingerprints. Then he set the weapon on the ground before hustling Carrie along the alley.

When they had turned a corner, putting another building between them and the scene of carnage, he called the safe house.

Gary Blain answered again. "Wyatt?"

"Yes. We got out of there. We're coming back. We won't have the town car."

"Thank God you're okay." He paused. "What about Collins?"

"He didn't make it."

Gary absorbed that bit of bad news, then asked, "What are you going to do for transportation?"

"There's a Zipcar agency a couple of blocks away. We can rent one of those."

"Be careful down there, man."

"I always am."

When he hung up, Carrie looked at him. "What's a Zipcar?"

"Cars you can rent by the hour. Like bicycles in Europe."

"I didn't know about that, either."

Probably a function of her living in a million-dollar condo in Columbia Heights with a spectacular view of the city. He was tempted to say something about her dad's money making it unnecessary for her to rent anything, but he decided there was no point in needling her. Not after they'd narrowly escaped getting killed—and after he'd seen what she was made of. He'd known she had the guts to turn in men plotting against the U.S. government. He hadn't known the rest.

"Are you going to call the police now?" she asked, breaking into his thoughts.

"We still can't trust them. We still don't have a handle on how those guys found out about your meeting. For all we know, the terrorists have a spy in the D.C. police department."

She winced. "How would that be possible?"

"It just takes one bad cop who wants to supplement his income."

"But he'd know he'd be setting us up to get killed."

"Some people will do just about anything for money. Do you know how many people got killed because Aldrich Ames, that turncoat in the CIA, blew their cover?"

"I don't know the exact number, but I get your point."

"Which means I'm not taking any chances," he answered as he led her down Tenth Street to the storefront with the Zipcar office.

The blond young man behind the counter, wearing a dress shirt and tie, looked up as they stepped in.

"We'd like a vehicle with four-wheel drive," Wyatt said.

Carrie looked surprised but said nothing.

"How long will you be needing it?"

"At least a day."

"There will be extra charges if you turn it in later."

"Understood."

"Driver's license?"

Beside him Carrie tensed. He touched her arm reassuringly, then dug into his wallet and pulled out an alternate ID.

He handed over a license that said he was Will Hanks.

The clerk filled out the paperwork, and they were out of the office and on the road in less than fifteen minutes.

Carrie sank into the passenger seat of the Chevy Equinox, leaned back against the headrest and closed her eyes. He watched her take a few moments to catch her breath before she turned to him. "You always carry fake ID?"

"Yeah." His gaze alternated between her and the road. "You did good back there."

"What choice did I have?"

"A lot of people would have gone to pieces or frozen up when the crap hit the fan. You didn't."

She huffed out a breath. "I guess I didn't go to pieces when I spotted those guys in the park, either."

"True."

She made a snorting sound. "One minute I was

taking pictures of a happy little eagle family. Then I was in the middle of an action-adventure movie."

"More real than 3-D."

"Yeah. When they shoot at you in a 3-D movie, you can't get killed."

He turned onto Connecticut Avenue and took that route toward the suburbs.

"Why did you get a four-wheel-drive car?" she asked.

"We might not be going in the front entrance to the safe house," he answered, then switched the subject. "I want to find out who ratted you out. Who knew about your meeting downtown?"

She sighed. "I did discuss it with my dad because he wanted to stay informed."

"He asked me questions about the meeting, too."

She turned her head toward him. "But he wouldn't tell anyone. He doesn't even trust the government. He hired you and your team because he wanted to keep me safe."

Wyatt nodded. "Other people are at his house. Someone might have heard."

"No one there would set me up like that."

Although Wyatt heard the note of conviction in her voice, he wasn't so sure. He'd be the judge of who might have betrayed Carrie. Right now, though, his primary goal was to get her back to safety, and he needed to make sure nobody was on their tail.

He wanted to speed back to the safe house, but he allowed himself to go no faster than five miles above the speed limit as he watched the rearview mirror for any signs that they were being followed. He saw none.

Pulling out his phone again, he dialed the secure number. This time he waited eight rings, but nobody picked up. A very bad sign.

Instead of leaving a message, he clicked off.

"What?" she asked.

"Nobody answered."

"What does that mean?"

"I don't know, and I don't like it."

They were on a secondary road that led through the rolling Maryland countryside. As he'd suggested he might do, he turned off onto a dirt track that circled the safe-house property, staying on the alert for signs of trouble.

"What are you doing?"

He gave her a quick look. "I'm not taking you in there until I know everything's all right."

"It's supposed to be secure. That's why it's called a safe house."

"And right now the vibes are all wrong."

"Then why are we going back at all?"

"A couple of reasons. There's equipment in there that I need. And the rest of the team could be in trouble."

THE NEWS OF the ambush at the Federal Building had hit the cable channels. Tuned in to the CNN broadcast, the watcher felt anger flare up. A lot of money had crossed hands—for results—and now it looked as though everything was going to hell in a handbasket.

After clicking off the TV, the individual walked down the hall, stepped into a darkened bedroom and dialed a cell phone number, hand tightening on the phone while waiting for someone on the other end of the line to pick up.

"Yes?"

The caller spoke in a low, steady voice, working hard to hold back screams. "What the hell is going on?"

"A glitch."

"You call that a glitch? The attack on the Federal Building has hit all the major news stations. The only bodies they found were that Federal prosecutor—what's his name—Skip Gunderson? And two of your guys. I assume that means the agent and the girl got away."

"Yeah. A real screwup."

"There better not be any blowback."

"The dead guys won't talk. And we got the rest of our men out before anyone else showed up."

"How did you make such a mess of a simple assignment?"

"You neglected to tell us how good Wyatt Hawk is."

"I'm as surprised as you are." The caller made a throat-clearing noise. "Where are Hawk and the girl?" Maybe that news would be better.

"We don't know for certain. We figure they'll come back to the safe house. We can get them there."

"You're sure?"

"It's a good bet."

"What if that doesn't work out?"

"We go to plan B."

"That's just perfect."

Before the caller could ask another question, the man on the other end of the line hung up, leaving nothing but dead air.

The caller had thought of a foolproof scheme. Apparently, that held true only if you weren't working with morons. More proof that if you wanted something done right, you'd better do it yourself. Too bad it took special training to handle this job.

FIFTY MINUTES AFTER leaving the Zipcar office, Wyatt pulled the Chevy Equinox into the woods, torn between bad and worse alternatives. He could leave Carrie in the car or hiding in the underbrush while he went in to find out what was going on at the hideout. Unfortunately, that would mean she was vulnerable if someone was lurking nearby. Or he could take her with him, which would expose her to whatever danger might be waiting ahead.

He made a decision and turned toward Carrie. "I don't want to leave you here unprotected. We're going to approach the house from the right side. I want you to stay behind me, and do exactly what I say. If I tell you to hit the deck, you do it." His gaze burned into hers. "Got that?"

"Yes."

"Wait in the car until I signal you to get out."

She answered with a tight nod.

Hoping he could count on her not to freeze up, he climbed out of the vehicle and checked the area before motioning for her to follow.

As they approached the property line, they came in low, making themselves as small a target as possible. The first real evidence that something was wrong hit Wyatt when they reached the electric fence. He threw a stone at it and was only half surprised to find that it was no longer working. Somehow the current to the wires had been disrupted.

He threw another stone, then took a chance and crept forward to touch the fence. Nothing happened. Dead as a drowned rat.

Again he considered leaving Carrie but decided against the tactic.

He was able to lift the wire fence and scoot under, then hold it for her.

She came up beside him, her gaze focused on the house.

"It's quiet," she whispered.

"Too quiet. You might think we'd hear the TV. Or guys talking."

Too bad he didn't have a pair of binoculars. But he hadn't anticipated the need to spy on a facility that had been perfectly safe when they'd left.

His instincts warned him to turn around and get the hell out of there, but he couldn't do it. Not when he felt an obligation to the men who'd taken this assignment with him. What if they were injured? Or being held under threat of death?

"Stay low," he whispered.

Carrie did as he'd asked.

Taking his time, he moved forward until they came to the flat stretch, where the fields for a hundred yards around the structure had been cleared to make it difficult for anyone to sneak up on the safe house. Great planning when you were on the inside, but not so advantageous if you were trying to get close to the house.

Unfortunately, he found he didn't have to get close to understand what had happened. The evidence was big as life and twice as plain—a body lying sprawled across the back steps.

Chapter Three

Carrie heard Wyatt mutter a curse.

Alarmed, she followed the direction of his gaze.

From her hiding place, she saw a dark-skinned man with a shaved head lying at the bottom of the back steps, his arms spread and a gun still clutched in his hand. As she realized who it was, her chest constricted painfully. The man was Gary Blain, one of the bodyguards who'd gone out of his way to be nice to her during guard duty. It looked as though he'd been trying to get away when he'd been gunned down.

She choked back a sob. Another casualty. On her account. "No."

Wyatt put his arm around her shoulder, pulling her against his side, and she turned toward him, closing her eyes and pressing her forehead against his chest.

"Well, we know why he didn't answer the phone," he said in a raspy voice.

"What about the rest of them?"

"We've got to assume they're dead, too. Probably in the house. And Gary almost got away."

"My fault—again," she whispered.

"No. The bastards are determined to get you. When we escaped from the Federal Building, they probably came here. Or maybe they sent a team here as a precaution in case we got out of the trap they'd set."

"How did they know about this place?"

"Obviously, somebody gave away this location."

"Could they have followed you? I mean, sometime earlier?"

"I don't think so," he answered, but she heard the tiny note of doubt in his voice. Still, he continued, "We have to assume it's the same person who told them about your meeting this morning."

Carrie fought the sick feeling rising in her throat. Death and destruction were following close on her heels. It was hard to imagine everything that had happened today and harder still to believe that someone was deliberately trying to kill her. But apparently, that was what happened when you ratted on terrorists.

"What are we going to do?" she murmured.

"For starters, thank God that we did't go charging in there."

"You mean thank your instincts."

"Whatever," he answered dismissively. "We'd better get the hell back to the car before somebody spots us."

Even as he spoke, it was already too late. Lookouts must have been stationed in all directions, because in the next second, gunfire erupted from inside the house, and men charged outside, sprinting in their direction.

Wyatt grabbed Carrie's hand, leading her back the way they'd come, heading for the screen of trees. Behind them she heard running feet closing the gap.

Lord, no.

"On my own turf, I've got a little surprise to slow them down," he said. He reached into his pocket, pulling out something that looked like a cell phone. As they ran, he pressed a series of buttons. In back of them, small explosions began to erupt from the grass, sending sprays of dirt and stones into the air.

She heard a loud curse, as someone behind them took a hit.

The explosions continued, but Wyatt didn't slow his pace, so she kept running beside him, her lungs burning as she struggled to keep up with him.

She was beginning to think they were in the clear when the gunfire stopped. But after the last explosion, she heard a sound that made the hair on her arms prickle. Someone must have escaped Wyatt's trap and he was pounding along behind them.

At first the thuds were faint. Whoever was back there had lost ground because of the charges, but he was catching up, and now he began shooting as he went.

Wyatt whirled and returned fire, but his weapon was no match for his opponent's. Unfortunately, they were still a long way from the electric fence and the car, and she could hear the pursuer steadily gaining on them.

She glanced at Wyatt, seeing the grim set of his jaw. Apparently, he didn't think they were going to make it to the fence.

When they came to a place where the land had been contoured into several small hills and valleys, Wyatt stopped.

"Get down. And stay down, no matter what happens."

She remembered when she hadn't liked Wyatt. Now she obeyed his orders without question, because she knew that was the only way she was getting out of this trap alive.

Dropping behind a hillock, she dragged in great gasps of air and pressed her hand against her side, her gaze fixed on the man who was charging toward them, firing his weapon as he ran.

She ducked and slung her arms over her head, as if that would stop a bullet. Her heart was pounding as she waited for Wyatt to drop the guy. But in the next moment, Wyatt made a strangled sound and fell back against the ground.

Carrie felt her heart stop. He'd been hit!

With a whoop of victory, the gunman closed the last few yards between them and swung his weapon toward her, taking a long moment to meet her terrified gaze.

"Don't," she whispered.

But Wyatt obviously had no intention of letting

her get murdered. He leaped from behind the mound and shot the guy in the back at point-blank range. The attacker went down with a gasp of surprise.

Wyatt charged toward her, snatching the assault rifle from the man's grasp.

"Why didn't you shoot him before he got so close?" she gasped as she stared at the terrorist. He was another perfectly normal-looking young man. If you saw him on the street, you never would have known what was in his mind.

"Because I only had one bullet left, and it had to count," Wyatt answered.

He turned to look back the way they'd come, and she followed his gaze toward the bodies of two men sprawled in the field. Neither was moving.

"Are they dead?"

"We can't go back to find out. Come on. Before another one comes after us," he said.

Reaching down a hand, he helped her up. She swayed on her feet for a moment. Then they ran back toward where they'd left the car. She was out of breath when they reached the fence, and he held it up for her. She dived beneath the wires, and he followed.

They made it to the vehicle, and she allowed relief to flood through her as she climbed in and locked the door. Wyatt shoved the weapon he'd appropriated onto the floor between his seat and the console, then turned the ignition and slammed the shift into Drive, speeding away before any other terrorists could figure out what had gone wrong with their foolproof plan.

She sat for a few moments gripping the edges of her seat, willing her heart to stop pounding and her breath to slow. Against all odds, they had gotten away again. Thanks to the man beside her.

"Are you okay?" he asked.

"Yes."

Then she remembered the sound he had made as the terrorist was charging toward them. When she opened her eyes and swung her gaze to the left, she saw the blood oozing through the fabric of his shirt.

"You really are hit," she gasped out. "You weren't just pretending to get his attention."

"It's not bad."

"How do you know?"

"I can move my arm all right. I can drive. The bone's not broken."

"You have to—"

"—get us the hell out of here before they figure out which way we went."

She saw the set of his jaw as he kept driving along the narrow country road, watched him grimace when he had to turn the wheel, putting distance between them and the safe house that was no longer a refuge.

She wanted to ask what they were going to do now, but she was sure he'd tell her when he figured it out. It was amazing how much her thinking had changed in the past few hours. She'd thought Wyatt was a grim lone wolf, and she had wondered why her father had hired him. Now she understood that he was the best man for the job. Maybe the only man. Could anyone else have saved her life so many times today?

She heard him curse under his breath, and alarm shot through her.

Jerking upright, she looked in all directions but saw no suspicious cars.

"What?"

"I shouldn't have gone back there," he muttered, and she knew he was blaming himself for the latest shoot-out.

"You had your reasons."

"They were a mistake."

He clenched his teeth, and she could tell he was fighting the pain in his arm. If she'd known where they were going, she would have ordered him to let her drive, but the safe house was in an isolated part of the county, accessible only from a series of narrow, winding roads, an area she barely knew.

All she could do was divide her attention between their surroundings and Wyatt, watching the sinister red patch on his sleeve grow bigger as he drove.

He saw her watching him. "It's not an artery."

"Glad to hear it."

"I'd already be dead if it were."

She made a snorting sound.

He kept driving, clenching his teeth every time he made a turn and checking the rearview mirror frequently to make sure they weren't being followed.

When signs of civilization began appearing, he slowed his speed. Finally they approached a strip mall, and he pulled into the parking lot of a drugstore, finding a spot near the door. "I'm going to stay here. Can you go in and get a few things?"

"Of course."

"I need gauze pads, antiseptic, adhesive tape, and if they have men's shirts, get me something I can wear that's not bloodstained."

She nodded and climbed out, looking around to make sure nobody was paying any attention.

Inside, she grabbed a shopping cart and took a moment to orient herself, then headed for the first-aid section. She found the required items and added a bottle of painkillers, a bottle of water and a roll of paper towels. Then she went to the clothing department. It wasn't large, but she did find a long-sleeved, button-down-the-front sports shirt that looked as if it would fit Wyatt.

At the cash register, she started to reach for her credit card, then remembered a credit transaction could be traced. Instead, she paid in cash and hurried back to the car. Wyatt was sitting with his head thrown back and his eyes closed. They snapped open, and his hand went to the gun when she opened the passenger door. When she realized it was her, he relaxed.

He'd gotten them to the shopping center, but now his skin was gray and covered with perspiration. He was in shock.

"You're not in any shape to drive," she said.

She expected an argument, but he got out of the car and walked unsteadily to her side. She switched places with him, then drove around the back of the shopping center.

He stared around in surprise. "What are you doing?"

"Having a look at your arm."

The strip mall backed up onto a wooded area, and she drove to the side of the blacktop, parking under some low-hanging maple trees.

"Let me get my shirt off."

He heaved himself up and climbed out, where he stood studying the area. When he established that they were alone, he started unbuttoning his shirt. She could see that moving his arm was hurting him.

Joining him, she said, "Let me."

Standing in front of him, she began working the buttons, exposing his broad chest, which was covered with a dark mat of hair and what looked like an old scar.

"What happened to you?" she asked as she gently touched the scar.

"I was in a war zone," he clipped out, telling her by his tone that he wanted her to drop the subject.

Pressing her lips together, she tried not to focus on his buff physique as she helped him take his good arm out of his sleeve, then gathered up the fabric so that she could ease the other sleeve down his arm. The blood had already stuck the fabric to his skin, and he made a small sound as she peeled the shirt away. There was a trash can nearby. Balling up the shirt, she started toward it.

He stopped her with a firm command. "No. I don't want any evidence left around here."

"Oh, right."

He walked back to the passenger seat and sat down heavily, giving her access to the arm. Gingerly, she examined the wound. It looked as if the bullet had torn a path across his skin, leaving a deep canyon in his flesh.

He turned his head and inspected the track. "It's not bad. Which is good, because spending time in an emergency room could be dangerous."

"Why?"

"That's a logical place to look for me."

"How would they know you were hurt?"

"I left some blood on the ground."

She made a low sound. She had been so wound up with getting away that she hadn't even noticed.

After opening the paper towels, she pulled a couple off, wadded them up and wet them with the water, then gingerly wiped at the dried blood on his arm, being careful not to start the wound bleeding again.

She'd barely spoken to the man in the week she'd been with him. In the space of a few hours, she'd gotten to know him a lot better. Now she felt the intimacy of this encounter. He was half-naked, and she was tending to him with hands-on closeness.

She might have tried to speed through the first aid. Instead, the situation made her want to linger. Too bad they were parked in the back of a shopping center, a location that wasn't exactly private.

"How did my father happen to hire you?" she asked.

"He was looking for someone to guard you, and he got a recommendation from one of my former bosses at the CIA. I guess he liked what he heard."

"You quit the Agency?"

"I got into a situation in Greece."

"What kind of situation?"

"I got my partner killed," he snapped.

"It probably was as much his fault as yours."

"Her."

"Oh."

"I should have known better than to get involved with her." The way he said it told her this was another subject he didn't want to talk about. She wouldn't press him. Not now when he was injured, although she couldn't help wondering what had happened.

She opened the bottle of antiseptic. "This may sting."

He answered with a tight nod.

She poured the clear liquid onto his arm, hearing him wince as it pooled in the wound.

When she was satisfied that she'd cleaned it well, she taped on the gauze pads.

Next came the shirt, which she pulled out of the bag and unbuttoned. Reversing the process, she helped him get his arms through the sleeves, which turned out to be about an inch too short, so she left the cuffs unbuttoned.

Before she finished, a blast from a car horn startled her, making her lose her balance and fall forward, pressing her breasts against Wyatt's face. Quickly she pushed herself away. Turning, she saw a white Jeep with an orange dome light on top. A middle-aged man in a security guard's uniform was leaning out the driver's window, staring at them with narrowed eyes.

"This side of the lot is for store owners and employees only. You can't come back here and make out," he said in a stern voice.

When she started to object that they'd been doing no such thing, Wyatt put a hand on her arm.

"Sorry, Officer," he said.

"Button up your shirt and move along."

"Yes, sir," Wyatt answered.

She'd never expected to hear him cave in the face of authority, and she knew he probably hated doing it, but she also knew he was avoiding any kind of confrontation, avoiding having the guy come over and see the bloodied shirt or the gun in the car. While Wyatt and the guard had exchanged pleasantries, she'd bundled the supplies back into the drugstore bag and thrown them in the backseat. Now she hurried around to the driver's door. The security guy stayed where he was while she pulled away, then followed her to the parking lot entrance. She waited for the light to change and pulled out, heading down the road in the opposite direction from where they'd come.

Wyatt had leaned back in his seat but now he sat up suddenly and cursed.

Carrie's gaze shot to him in alarm. "What?"

"We have to get rid of that gun."

"Like throw it in the bushes?"

"No. Like put it in the trunk."

He craned his neck to look at a road sign. "Turn off on a side road and look for a place where there aren't any houses."

She followed directions, and they both got out. She blocked the view from the road while he stowed the weapon out of sight.

Back in the car, he directed her to the Intercounty Connector. When they'd gotten onto the high-speed road that cut across the D.C. area, he said, "Get off at Route 29 and head for Columbia. There are a lot of motels over there. Find something that's part of a midpriced chain."

When they reached Route 29, she slowed, and he looked at her inquiringly. "What are you doing?"

"I have to call my father and tell him I'm okay."

"When we know we're safe."

"He'll be worried."

"We'll be in Columbia in less than thirty-five minutes. If you were dead, he'd know it. The news stations would have already broadcasted it."

She winced.

He leaned back and closed his eyes, and she took the highway he'd suggested, which turned out to be a toll road that cut across Montgomery County to Howard County.

ALTHOUGH THE SAFE house had been deemed an easy target, four men had been given the job of taking it down and waiting for Carrie and Wyatt to return. Now two of the men were dead and one was wounded. The guy who was still functional walked down the access road and into the woods, where he and his partners had parked a white van out of sight. The standard anonymous utility vehicle. In this case, perfectly suitable for getting rid of the bodies of three large men who'd been at the wrong place at the wrong time. And two terrorists who'd gotten themselves killed by taking off after the fleeing man and woman.

The four-man team had caught the hired guards by surprise because the bitch they'd been minding had been out of the house, which was reason enough for them to relax. The unwanted visitors had disabled the security system at the safe house—as a further means of gaining access unawares. Nobody had been looking out the windows when they'd crept up through the fields and made the dash across the cleared land around the house. Only one of the guards inside had been on his toes enough to make it outside, and he hadn't gotten any farther than the back steps. Too bad his body had alerted the guy with Carrie Mitchell that something was wrong at the house. And too bad he'd come sneaking up from the side yard. Apparently, he was an efficient and cautious fellow.

The men who'd taken the house were named Harry, Sidney, Jordan and Bruce. Sid was the only one not wounded or killed.

He wished he'd turned down the job. He hadn't signed up for this gig because of any ideological convictions. He was in it strictly for the cash. Now he was cursing himself for getting lured in by easy money. It flitted through his mind to climb in the van and drive away. Then keep driving. He already had the first payment from the patron who'd hired him and the others.

But he didn't think escape was a practical solution. You didn't just quit a job like this. Once you were in, you were in for the duration. And from where he was sitting now, it looked as though it was going to be a longer haul than he'd been led to believe. The only way they were getting out of this was to finish the mission—or die trying. Harry and Jordan were already dead. And Bruce had a mangled leg. Two of the guys in the downtown end of the operation had also bought the farm.

Although Carrie Mitchell and her bodyguard had made it out of the area, Sid didn't call in for instructions right away. Instead, he spread tarps in the back of the van and started the annoying process of loading the five bodies into the vehicle before cleaning up the blood on the floor inside the house and moving dirt around to cover the blood outside, as per the instructions he'd been given to leave as little evidence as possible.

Bruce watched him work with dull eyes. Usually he was the one in charge. Now he was in too bad a shape to do more than nurse his wounded leg. "I'm hurt bad, man," he moaned.

"We'll get you back to headquarters."

"Shouldn't I be in the hospital?"

Sid gave him a considering look. "Hang on. That's what you'd say to me if our situations were reversed."

"It's a long way back to the hideout."

"Not that far, and it's real private."

Bruce cringed, probably thinking that his partner was considering leaving him in the same condition as the bodies. He closed his mouth and let Sid finish the quick and dirty cleanup. The rushed job wouldn't hide the evidence if the cops came in with luminol. But it was probably going to be a long time—if ever—before the authorities got to the safe house.

Who was going to call them? Not Wyatt Hawk. He was too conscious of maintaining the secrecy of his assignment. Which was going to make it difficult to find him and the woman. Hopefully, plan B would flush them out. And hopefully Sid could go back to his normal life of petty crime.

Chapter Four

As Carrie drove toward Columbia, she glanced at Wyatt. He was sitting with his head back and his eyes closed. She wanted to reach out and press the back of her hand to his cheek, but she had the feeling that if she did, he'd come instantly alert, and she'd find a gun pointed at her side. Which meant it was prudent to keep her hands on the wheel.

She knew Wyatt was being cautious when he'd asked her to drive so far away from the safe house. Would the terrorists really start checking every motel within a twenty-mile radius of their last known location? She doubted it, with so many motels in this area. But maybe they'd do it if they were desperate enough. And they'd certainly seemed determined to stop her from testifying.

Beside her Wyatt made a strangled sound, and her eyes snapped to him, seeing him looking around and getting his bearings.

"How are you feeling?" she asked.

"Okay."

Probably it was a lie—designed to reassure her. How could he feel okay after getting shot?

He shook his head and started to stretch, then stopped abruptly, undoubtedly because the pain in his arm had hit him. He dragged in a breath and let it out.

"How long was I sleeping?"

"A half hour."

"How close are we to Columbia?"

"We're here, but I don't know where to find a motel. They built the place so you can't find anything."

He laughed. "It was the original plan not to spoil the view with big signs. Then they realized that they needed to make the commercial areas more obvious." He looked around. "Head down Route 108, then turn at the Palace Nine shopping center. You'll find the right kind of motels along 100 Parkway."

She took his advice, stopping at a chain that advertised breakfast along with a room for less than a hundred bucks a night.

"You stay here. I'll check in," he said.

"Why?"

"Because I don't want the clerk to see a man and a woman together and remember the two of us if anyone comes asking questions. And a lone male is less suspicious than a lone female."

She nodded and pulled into a parking space near the door. When he got out, she watched him steady himself against the car door, then square his shoulders.

She gave him a critical inspection as he headed for the lobby. He looked like a guy who wasn't feeling 100 percent, but there was no way to know that he'd been shot a little more than an hour ago.

She glanced around, glad to see that nobody was paying her any particular attention.

PATRICK HARRISON STRUGGLED not to let his taut nerves overwhelm him. He spared a quick glance at his watch. It had been two hours since he and Carrie's father had heard the news of the attack in Washington, D.C., and he felt the tension humming around the comfortable, wood-paneled home office.

He sat in one of the leather guest chairs. Douglas Mitchell sat behind his broad rosewood desk. They were both staring at a flat-screen television tuned to CNN. There had been nothing new to report for the past hour and a half, but the commentators were attempting to fill the air. At the moment the network was running a background piece on the Mitchell family, discussing the way Douglas Mitchell had taken the twenty million dollars he'd inherited from his father and turned it into over a billion—by buying up companies in distress and gutting them. The tactic had made him popular with the investment group he'd formed but not so much with the men and women who'd lost their jobs under his tender loving care.

Next came candid shots of Carrie as a teenager riding in horse shows and more shots of her all grown up and out on dates in D.C. with various eligible bachelors. She was also shown with her father on a trip to Europe they'd taken two years ago. There were no shots of Patrick, of course. He was invisible as far as the family history was concerned.

Next were some of the nature pictures Carrie had taken close to home and across the U.S. Patrick realized that if she survived this ordeal, her career was going to get a big boost. Or if she died, perhaps her pictures would sell for hundreds of dollars more than they had the day before.

Patrick shot a glance at Douglas's rigid profile. The man had one hand pressed to his forehead as though trying to ward off a headache.

Patrick tried to make his voice reassuring. "Carrie's in good hands. I'm sure she got away."

Douglas whirled around in his swivel chair, his eyes fierce. "I'm not interested in your half-assed opinion. You don't have any more information than I do." He was as wired as a cat caught in a clothes dryer. Of course, he had a right to be. Since the moment his daughter had come home to the Mitchell estate to tell him about overhearing a terrorist plot, he'd been sick with worry about her.

Not that you could tell what he was feeling, unless you knew him well enough to see below the surface of his bluff exterior.

His attitude came across as annoyance and anger,

but Patrick had been with him long enough to understand the old man's anxiety. His daughter had come forward to testify against a gang of domestic terrorists, putting herself in immediate danger. She'd been hiding out for a week, and she'd gone downtown to meet with the Federal prosecutor. Unfortunately, the terrorists had been waiting for her and her bodyguard, Wyatt Hawk.

From the news accounts, it seemed that Hawk had gotten her out of the building. But where were they now?

Patrick took a calming breath. He'd known Carrie all his life, and he hated feeling as though there was nothing he could do, but he didn't see any effective course of action open to him.

The old man picked up his phone and punched in Hawk's cell number once again. The results were the same as every other time Douglas had tried to make the call. There was no answer.

"Damn him!" the elder Mitchell growled. For a moment, it looked as if he would throw the phone across the room.

"Remember your blood pressure," Patrick murmured.

"I don't need your damn advice," Mitchell shot back, slapping his hand against the desk. After a moment, he took a breath and said, "Sorry. I'm on edge. I shouldn't take it out on you."

"I understand."

"But I need to know what's going on." This time

he dialed the safe house where Carrie had been staying for the past week. The results were the same.

"What can I do to help?" Patrick asked.

"Bring me a scotch and soda."

"Is that wise?"

"Don't question me."

Patrick sighed and got up. Again he sneaked a glance at his watch. How long was this ordeal going to last?

Maybe he could have a drink, too. And maybe he'd have another discussion with Douglas about hiring security for himself, although the man was firm in his conviction that he didn't need it.

He had just crossed the thick carpet to the bar when a noise alerted him that something was wrong. He whipped around to see two men standing in the office doorway. They wore ski masks over their faces and carried automatic weapons.

Patrick leaped toward the desk, putting himself between Douglas and the two men.

"What the hell?" Douglas turned.

"Out of the way." One of the men charged toward Patrick and hit him on the side of the head with the butt of a gun. He cried out in pain and went down, struggling to cling to consciousness.

While he was on the floor, the other intruder crossed to Douglas Mitchell. "Come on."

"Where?"

"You'll find out." The man grabbed Douglas by the arms and hustled him toward the door. When

Douglas struggled, the man shoved a gun into the older man's back. "Cooperate, or you're going to get killed."

The man turned to address Patrick. "Tell Carrie Mitchell that if she doesn't turn herself in, her father's dead."

"We...we haven't heard from her," he managed to say.

"Well, you'd better hope she calls. And oh, yeah, if you contact the cops, you can kiss Mitchell's ass goodbye."

THE LONGER CARRIE waited for Wyatt to come out of the motel office, the more her tension grew. So many bad things had happened in the past few hours that she couldn't stop herself from waiting for the next one.

To her relief, Wyatt returned with the key in under five minutes and directed her to a room around back. One room. She didn't love that arrangement, but she understood why he'd done it.

Inside, the accommodations were pretty standard, with two queen-size beds and enough room so that they could keep out of each other's way.

Wyatt pulled back the spread on one of the beds, kicked off his shoes and lay down heavily.

"I'm going to call my father," she said.

"Go ahead."

She dug her phone out of her purse and clicked it on. It beeped immediately.

"There are messages for me."

"Call your father first," he said as he leaned back against the pillow and closed his eyes.

"Right." She clicked the automatic-dial button for her father's house. The call was answered on the first ring, not by Douglas Mitchell. It was Patrick Harrison, her father's chief of staff. His mother had been a maid in their house, and she'd died in an automobile accident twenty-five years earlier. Since there had been no relatives willing to take the three-year-old boy, her father had unofficially adopted Patrick, and he'd been a member of the household ever since. He'd gone to college at Ohio State, then come back home to work for the senior Mitchell.

"Carrie, thank God," he said. "I've been trying to call you, but there was no answer." He sounded near hysterical.

She kept her own voice calm as she answered, "Wyatt told me to turn off my phone so they couldn't use it to pinpoint our location."

"Are you all right?"

"Yes. But the men at the safe house are dead." She gulped. "All except Wyatt. We were going back there, but it was an ambush. Like at the Federal Building."

"Thank God you're all right," he said again.

Something in the tone of his voice told her he wasn't just worried about her.

"What happened?" she asked, praying that her father hadn't had a heart attack or a stroke.

"There's no easy way to say this."

"Then spit it out!"

"Your father's been kidnapped."

"Lord, no!"

At the sound of her raised voice, Wyatt surged off the bed. Crossing to her, he took the phone out of her hand.

"What did you just tell Carrie?" he demanded, clicking on the speaker so that they could both hear.

"Her father's been kidnapped."

"How? Where?"

"Two men came to the house."

"Are you all right?" Carrie interjected.

"One of them hit me with the butt of his gun, but I'm okay. They're demanding that Carrie turn herself in, or they'll kill Douglas. And they said they'll kill him if I call the police."

Carrie gasped, hardly able to believe what she'd just heard.

"Are you sure it's the terrorists?" Wyatt demanded.

"I...guess. I don't know for sure. Who else would they be?"

"What did they look like?"

"They were wearing ski masks."

"Is there anything else you can tell me?"

"I was on the floor, hanging on to consciousness by my fingernails."

Carrie made a low sound. "I'm so sorry."

"It's okay. I mean, I'm still here. Maybe so I could give you the message about your father."

"Yeah," Wyatt agreed.

Patrick switched subjects. "Where are you?"

"Somewhere safe," Wyatt answered.

"We have to go home," Carrie said.

"No." Wyatt fixed his gaze on her. "Patrick just said that men broke in and took your father, but they want you. They'll keep him alive as long as they don't have you. If you turn yourself in, you're dead, and so is he."

Carrie stared at Wyatt. A few minutes ago he had seemed as if he needed a good night's rest before he would be fully functional. Now he looked like the agent in charge again. "I want to know what happened, but I'm not going to take that information now, in case this call is being traced."

"By whom?" Patrick asked.

"The terrorists. I'll call you back soon."

"But—"

Wyatt clicked off.

ON THE OTHER end of the line, Patrick Harrison cursed. Slamming down the phone, he stood for a moment, struggling to control his temper as he reminded himself to breathe in and out slowly. Hawk had said he would call back. When, exactly?

Patrick had just been through a terrible ordeal, and now he didn't like the way Wyatt Hawk was handling the situation. No, for starters, he didn't like it that Hawk was on the case at all.

Patrick had come up with the initial list of bodyguards. Then he'd found something questionable in the guy's background. He'd told Douglas not to hire Hawk, but the man had always had a mind of his own. He might listen to advice, then do the exact opposite because he was sure he knew better. In this case, he'd decided to go ahead with the former CIA operative, even though the man had messed up on his last job.

Patrick had lived with Douglas Mitchell's arbitrary decisions for years. Since he'd come back from college to work for the old man, he'd thought more than once that he should have struck out on his own. But he'd been comfortable here, and when Douglas had made him a good offer, he'd known that the man wanted him to stay—and valued his work ethic.

But he'd found out soon enough that working for Douglas could be an exercise in frustration. Never more than at this moment. He'd have liked to have Carrie home at the family compound so he'd know exactly where she was. But Hawk had her stashed Lord knew where. It could be somewhere close. Or they could be in the next state by now.

He banged his fist against the rosewood desk, then struggled for calm again. Hawk had said he'd call back. Then Patrick would get more information. Or not, depending on Hawk's mood.

He cursed again, more softly this time. Wyatt Hawk was turning out to be the biggest mistake he could imagine making.

CARRIE'S STOMACH ROILED as she stood in the middle of the room, clutching her cell phone. "My father—"

"—is a hostage."

"Which is my fault. And the men who snatched him hurt Patrick."

"Carrie, none of this is your fault. You were just doing your duty as a citizen. What were you going to do, let them blow up the U.S. Capitol and pretend you hadn't heard anything?"

When she started to protest, Wyatt reached for her and pulled her close, pressing her face to his shoulder. "We have two jobs here. The first one is to keep you safe. The second is to get your dad back."

"What if I think that's the wrong order?" she asked in a strained voice.

"It's not. And we *will* get him back."

"How?"

His tone was soothing as he rubbed her back. "We don't do it by running off without a plan. We've got to consider all the angles and proceed carefully."

He kept his arms around her, rubbing her neck and shoulders, and she leaned into his strength as she thought back over the awful conversation with Patrick. Thank goodness she hadn't been alone. If Wyatt hadn't stopped her, she would probably have told Patrick where she was, and the terrorists could be on their way to the motel already if they'd been listening.

"They can't find us through the phone?" she murmured.

"We didn't speak long enough for them to trace the call. But I want to get rid of both our phones so they can't use the GPS."

She nodded against his shoulder.

"Are you feeling better?" he asked.

"Shouldn't that be my line?"

He managed a low laugh. "I'm fine."

"You were shot a little while ago. You were resting when I got ahold of Patrick."

"I've been hurt before, a lot worse than this."

"That scar on your chest."

"Yes."

"And you were in the hospital, right?"

"I said it was worse than this." He eased away from her. "We need to get a couple of prepaid phones so we can use them and throw them away."

"Okay."

He gave Carrie a direct look. "You trust Patrick?"

"Of course!"

"Who else is at your house?"

She thought for a moment. "There's Inez, our maid."

"How long has she been with you?"

"Fifteen years."

"Does she need money?"

"Everybody needs money."

He nodded. "Who else could have heard you talking to your father about your plans to hide out?"

She felt as if she was being interrogated, but she knew he needed to know the answers. "There's a gardening crew that comes by a couple of times a week. They could have been eavesdropping."

"Anyone else?"

"Not on a regular basis."

His eyes narrowed, and she could see he was considering contingencies. "I don't want to leave you here, and I don't want to take you to the store, but I think that sticking together is better at the moment."

She nodded, assuming he was probably afraid she'd call Patrick if he left her.

He carried the cell phones to the bathroom and crushed them under his heel, then stuffed the pieces into his pocket.

She winced, thinking about the contacts and the pictures he'd just destroyed.

He glanced at her, apparently reading her expression. "You can get a new one later."

"Right."

"I'm going out first." He opened the door and looked out, then crossed to the car and motioned for her to follow.

As she got in the car, she asked, "They couldn't have found us here already, could they?"

"Probably not, but I didn't think they would show up at the safe house before we got back there.

It appears that this operation is bigger and better organized than we assumed initially."

"Oh, great."

Minutes after they'd entered the motel room, they were back on the road.

This time, Wyatt took the driver's side. She wanted to protest that he should be resting, but she was pretty sure he wouldn't pay any attention to the suggestion. Obviously he was the kind of man who wasn't going to let a woman drive him unless he was incapacitated.

As he drove, he tossed away the pieces of the phones, then turned to her. "I have Patrick's bio. He's been with you for twenty-five years, right?"

"Yes."

"And does he have any reasons to dislike your family?"

"Why would he? My father did everything for him. He treated him like a son, actually. He had a bedroom down the hall from me. He ate all his meals with us. My father sent him to the same private school I went to. He paid his tuition at Ohio State."

"So he was a good student?"

"Yes."

"Did he ever give your father any trouble?"

"You mean like rebelling?"

"Yes."

"He and I did a couple of stupid things—like borrow my dad's car when we were both fifteen."

"What happened when your dad found out?"

"He didn't. We covered for each other."

"You like him?"

"He was as close to me as a brother." Memories flooded her. "We hung out together, because Dad was usually busy. You could say he was the kind of father who didn't have a lot of time for his kids, but I knew he loved me."

"We were talking about Patrick, not your dad."

"I was trying to explain why Patrick and I were so close."

"And he loved Patrick?"

She hesitated. "That might be too strong a word. I know he's fond of him. And he's certainly come to rely on him." Again she paused before continuing. "Patrick didn't have to come back and work for Dad, but he did that on his own."

"Okay." Wyatt checked the rearview mirror. "What about your mother?"

"Dad never talks about her."

"When's the last time you saw her?"

She thought for a moment. "When I was maybe six. I went into her room, and she was packing." The pain and confusion of that long-ago moment came zinging back to her again. "She said she loved me, but she needed to leave. She said she'd be back to see me, but she never came back."

"Why?"

"At the time I thought she'd abandoned me. Now I think my dad kept her away. I heard him and his lawyer talking once. Dad said that he'd given her a lot of money, and he wasn't springing for any more."

"Why do you think she left?"

"I think Dad was more wound up with his work than he was with her."

"Like with you and Patrick?"

"Yes."

"Could she be holding a grudge? Could she be angry enough to…try to hurt him?"

Carrie turned her head toward Wyatt. "Wait a minute. What are you trying to say? That my father wasn't kidnapped because of a terrorist plot?"

"I'm trying to look at every angle. Were you ever romantically involved with Patrick?" he asked.

The question startled her. "What business is that of yours?"

"I'm trying to understand the family dynamics."

"Patrick and I were never close that way," she clipped out, hoping he'd drop the subject, but apparently, he wasn't ready to do that.

"Did he ever try anything—and you rebuffed him?"

She sat perfectly still, remembering.

"From the look on your face, I take it the answer is yes."

"Once, at the pool, he came up behind me and put his arms around me."

"What did you do?"

"I swam away."

"How did he take that?"

"He never…tried again."

"How old were you?"

"We were teenagers. Would you drop it now?"

"Okay," he said, although she gathered from the tone of his voice that he wanted to keep interrogating her.

THIRTY MILES AWAY, things were unraveling for a key player in the unfolding drama.

The phone rang. And the caller ID said the number was unpublished.

Just let it ring, an interior voice advised. But that could turn out to be worse than picking it up.

Still, the hand that lifted the receiver wasn't quite steady.

"Hello?"

"You know who this is?"

"Yes."

"You're late on your payment."

"I'll have it in a few days."

"That's what you said last time."

"I swear I'll have it."

"You can't keep relying on our goodwill."

The line went dead, and the hand that replaced the receiver was shaking so hard that the instrument rattled.

Was there any way out of this? There had to be.

Chapter Five

"Tell me why someone else besides the terrorists could have kidnapped my father," Carrie said.

She watched Wyatt heave in a sigh and let it out before answering.

"It's all over the news. Someone could have taken advantage of the plot to go after him when he's vulnerable."

"Why?"

"That's what I'm trying to figure out. What do you know about his enemies?"

She didn't like the way he'd put that. He'd flat-out assumed that there were people who wanted to hurt her father.

"He didn't talk to me a lot about his business."

"But you do know something."

"He and a guy named Quincy Sumner had a pretty public fight over a piece of land they both wanted."

"And your father won."

"Yes."

"We'll put Sumner on our list. Where does he live?"

"Fairfax, Virginia."

They had arrived at the drugstore. This time they went in together. After buying four cell phones, Wyatt took Carrie on a quick run through the cosmetics and toiletries departments, where they bought some of the basics that they'd been forced to abandon at the safe house. He also bought her a sun hat. When he'd removed the tag, he put it on her head, pulling it down firmly to cover part of her face.

As they returned to the parking lot, he turned to her. "I'm going to call Patrick back, but I want to do the talking."

"What if I want to talk to him?"

"Let me deal with him. I'll put on the speaker so you can hear."

She gave a little nod. She didn't like it, but it was probably the best course, given the state of her emotions.

On the prepaid phone Wyatt dialed the Mitchell house.

Patrick picked up immediately.

"Where the hell have you been?" he demanded.

"Getting phones. Tell us what happened."

"Is Carrie there?"

"Yes," she answered, then forgot all about letting Wyatt handle the call. "When did you find out I was in trouble?"

"Your dad got a computer alert about a shoot-out in the Federal Building. He turned on the television, and we were both watching, so we didn't hear anything until armed men appeared in his office and threatened to kill him."

Carrie moaned. "Was he all right?"

He repeated what he'd said earlier. "I told you I was on the floor at the time. I couldn't see much, but he walked out under his own power. They said they'd exchange him for you."

"Surrendering to them would be foolish," Wyatt snapped.

"Then what are you going to do?" Patrick asked.

"I'll get back to you on that."

"If you come home, we can work together on this."

"You're kidding, right?" Wyatt said. "You just told me that they strolled into the house. It's not safe for Carrie there."

Patrick made a frustrated sound. "I guess you're right." Then he asked again, "Where are you?"

"It's safer if you don't know. What if they came back and tortured you for information?"

"I wouldn't talk."

Wyatt answered with a mirthless laugh. "Everybody talks when they're in enough pain."

"I have to know Carrie's going to be okay."

"I am," she answered, the response automatic. She wasn't okay, but she was still alive, thanks to Wyatt Hawk.

Patrick's voice was an unwelcome counterpoint to her thoughts.

"You need more protection," he said.

Before she could answer, Wyatt jumped back into

the conversation. "Like I said, that didn't work out so well last time."

"We need to discuss this," Patrick countered.

"There's nothing to discuss. You're not in charge of keeping Carrie safe."

"I could fire you."

Wyatt laughed. "I work for Douglas Mitchell, not you, and we're getting off now."

"Wait. When will I hear from you again?"

"I don't know."

"What if the kidnappers call?"

"Tell them to email me." Wyatt gave an email address.

"I may need to get in touch with you."

"You can use the same method."

"I may need to have quicker access."

"I'll keep checking my mail."

He clicked off before Patrick could ask another question.

Carrie closed her eyes and leaned back in her seat. "If you're guessing wrong, they could kill my dad."

"I don't think they will."

"But you're not sure."

"I'm sorry. We can't be absolutely sure of anything—except that they want you dead, and they'll try any method to get to you."

"My dad's health isn't that great. I was already worried that the stress of my being in danger would give him a heart attack or a stroke."

"Sorry," he said again. "My job is protecting you, and taking you home isn't the way to do it."

She gave him a direct look—and the only answer that made any sense. "I understand." After a moment, she added, "You said Patrick could email you, but you left your laptop back at the safe house, and you can't get mail on a cheap disposable phone, can you?"

"No, but I'm going to get another computer now. Then we'll pick up some clothes."

She could see he was thinking several steps ahead, while she was just trying to keep her nose above water.

Their next stop was one of the big computer and appliances chains, where Wyatt bought a midpriced laptop, using the credit card with the fake identity. Nearby was a discount department store where they each bought underwear and a couple of changes of clothing. He also bought Carrie a pair of sunglasses.

"This is costing you a lot," Carrie observed.

"Your dad can add it to the bill when we get him back."

She didn't bother saying she wasn't positive of that outcome.

By the time they were finished with the shopping expedition, Carrie was feeling worn-out. And she couldn't imagine how Wyatt was holding up. His wound might not be life-threatening, but it should have been more than enough to slow him down.

"We should eat something," he said.

She wasn't hungry, and she'd been feeling tense the whole time they were in the department store.

"We should call Patrick again," she said.

"I'd rather communicate by email."

"You said these phones can't be traced."

"Someone could have tapped into the phone system at your father's house. I'd rather not give them any information."

She sighed. "You have to set up that computer before you can get mail."

He nodded. "We can pick up dinner and eat in the room. That will save time. What do you want?"

She shrugged. "It's hard to think about food."

"But we both need to fuel up, with something simple and basic."

He drove to a fast-food burger chain and ordered loaded burgers, French fries and milk shakes for both of them. After getting the food at the drive-through window, they headed back to the motel, where he made a survey of the parking lot before pulling into the space in front of their unit.

She was still feeling wired, but she knew she needed to eat. After unpacking the food, she sat at the table, nibbling on the burger.

"Drink the milk shake," Wyatt advised. "You can use the calories."

She took a dutiful sip and found that she wanted more. Wyatt sat down across from her, interspersing eating and sipping with setting up his computer.

The room had a flat-screen television, and she

picked up the remote and turned on CNN. The content of the broadcast gave her a shock. It was all about Carrie Mitchell.

She watched in fascination as they showed the Federal Building where the ambush had taken place, then old pictures of her and even some of her friends talking about her.

One was Pam Simmons, who had ridden in horse shows with her. Another was an editor who'd bought some of her nature photos.

She studied the pictures of herself. Most of them were old. And in all of them her hair was different from the way it looked now, which was good. A shot of her standing with her father made her heart squeeze. She must have made some kind of sound, because she looked up to find Wyatt watching her.

"I'm a celebrity."

"Unfortunately."

"I had no idea I would attract so much attention."

"The shooting's big news. Bigger than the original terrorist plot."

"Why?"

"You foiled the plot, making it a nonevent. The shooting's the real deal."

She sighed.

"You really want to keep watching that?" he asked when a shot they'd seen before flashed on the screen again.

"I guess not." She flicked off the television, then switched her attention to Wyatt, studying his face for signs that he was in pain and seeing what he probably wanted to hide. "How's your arm?"

"It's been better." He went back to work, and she watched him from under lowered lashes. He was competent and efficient. She'd seen that from the beginning. She hadn't understood his level of commitment to her. Or was that just part of the job? She hoped it was more than that.

"I can get my mail now," he finally said.

She waited, feeling her heart rate accelerate, while he accessed the mail system.

"There's a message from Patrick. Marked *urgent*."

"What does it say?"

"'The terrorists contacted me. They said—'"

Before he could finish, she grabbed the laptop and turned it toward her. "'—*ask Carrie Mitchell if she wants to be responsible for her father's death.*'"

THE WORDS BURNED into Carrie's mind and soul. She leaped up and charged around the table, heading for the bag with the phones.

Wyatt was on his feet seconds behind her, stopping her as she grabbed for one of them. He took it out of her hand before she could switch it on. "Don't."

"I have to call him."

"That's what they want. That's why they set this up. It sounds like the phone at your father's place is almost certainly tapped."

"I can't stand by and let them kill him."

"They won't."

She gave him a fierce look. "You keep saying that, but he's not *your* father. He's mine, and I'm not going to be responsible for killing him."

"You won't be."

The stress of the day was suddenly too much for her. She'd held herself together until this moment. Now she felt hot tears well in her eyes.

Wyatt saw them. Lifting her into his arms, he carried her to one of the beds, leaning over to lay her gently down. When she saw him looking at her, she rolled away from him, curling into a ball, embarrassed that he was seeing her go to pieces.

He muttered something she couldn't hear. She felt him ease onto the bed and reach for her. Turning her toward him, he took her in his arms.

She hated crying in front of him, hated this whole situation, but she was too stressed out to contain the sobs that wracked her body.

Carrie had learned not to show her emotions. When she'd cried in front of her father, he'd gotten angry or annoyed and told her to "grow up." His attitude had pushed her away. She'd tried to act like she didn't need him, which was perhaps why she felt so devastated by his getting kidnapped. Maybe she was feeling guilty because their relationship had never been filled with the warm, fuzzy father-daughter moments that she saw in sitcoms. Or maybe nobody had that, and it was simply a Hollywood illusion.

And speaking of illusions, what about the way

she felt in Wyatt's arms now? Warm and safe. Perhaps even cherished. Or was she making that part up because of the way he held her and stroked her?

She didn't move away when her sobs subsided. Neither did he. He kept her close, stroking his hands over her back, brushing his lips against her hairline.

The light kiss stunned her. This man who had held himself aloof was trailing his lips against her face.

For most of their short acquaintance, she had told herself that she didn't like Wyatt Hawk, that she didn't need him. But everything had changed with the first blast from the man pretending to be a security guard at the Federal office building.

Wyatt had shot him dead. He'd gotten her out of the car and into the building, under fire. And that had only been the first time he'd saved her.

Now she felt emotions rushing through her.

They flip-flopped as he eased away from her, then stood, running a hand through his hair.

"I'm sorry. That was inappropriate," he said.

She didn't know what to say. Was it? Or had she invited intimacy without realizing it?

She took her lower lip between her teeth. Maybe he was right. Maybe he was doing her a favor by getting off the bed, although it certainly didn't feel like it at the moment.

"We should try to figure out who blew the whistle on your meeting," he said.

"Who do you think it is?"

"I've got an idea where to start."

DOUGLAS MITCHELL'S EYES blinked open. He couldn't see much because he was in a darkened room. But he knew he was lying on a narrow bed, like something in a child's room, only not as comfortable.

He felt disoriented, but that was nothing new. He'd been feeling this way for the past six months, hiding his fuzzy thinking because he didn't want to admit anything was wrong with him.

He moved his left hand, tugging at the cold metal around his wrist. When he tried to move his arm off the bed, something stopped him. A rope, he thought, but he couldn't be sure in the dark.

He closed his eyes again, trying to breathe evenly, trying to calm himself. If he got too upset, his blood pressure would go up, and he might have a stroke. That wouldn't do him any good—or Carrie, either.

He took blood-pressure medication and a whole bunch of other pills. He didn't think the men who were holding him captive had brought his pills.

But why would they? They were going to kill him anyway.

That thought sent a frisson of fear rippling through his mind.

He fought to calm himself.

Think!

Could he get away? Trick them somehow?

He didn't know, but he had to try. For Carrie.

His heart constricted when he thought about his daughter. She was so brave. So together. He'd never told her how much he loved her or how much he admired the way she'd taken charge of her life. Now he might never have the chance.

He pushed that thought away and tried to focus on what he needed to do.

But thoughts swam in and out of his head the way they often did these days.

He could almost remember when the fuzzy feeling had started. Almost, but not quite.

But he wouldn't give in to the brain fog. He had to keep going, projecting the iron will that had always stood him so well.

Thank the Lord he'd had Patrick to help him keep his finances straight—and make decisions about Carrie.

Patrick had combed through a list of security experts and picked Wyatt Hawk to keep Carrie safe. No, wait. Patrick hadn't picked Hawk. He'd recommended someone else. But Douglas had thought Hawk was better. Had that been a mistake?

He cursed under his breath. Had he made a foolish decision that had jeopardized his daughter's life?

He went from cursing to praying. He hadn't prayed in years, not for himself. But he could pray for Carrie, couldn't he?

She must still be safe. Or why would these men be holding him captive?

He wasn't sure about that. He wasn't sure about anything beyond his hostage status.

When the doorknob turned, he closed his eyes and pretended to sleep.

A shaft of light fell across his face, and he heard men talking.

"How long do we have to keep the old guy?"

"Until we know the daughter's taken care of. Then we can wash our hands of him."

"She won't know the difference if we off him now."

"That's against the boss's orders."

The door closed again, but the men must have been standing right on the other side because Douglas could still hear their voices. He strained to hear the rest of the conversation.

"The boss is a pain in the ass."

"Yeah. But we're getting paid enough to put up with it. We already got a payment."

"Not enough. I want more of it now. As a gesture of good faith, you know."

The voices faded away, and Douglas sat up in the bed. Had he really heard that conversation, or had he made it up to fit the situation? In his current state, he honestly didn't know.

CARRIE LAY WHERE Wyatt had left her on the bed. She'd thought about curling her body away from him. Instead, she'd kept her gaze on him as he walked into the bathroom and splashed cold water on his face, then walked to the table and pulled his computer toward him.

She'd almost gotten in over her head with him a few moments ago. But he'd done her a favor by pulling away.

Or *was* it a favor?

She felt too confused to make up her mind about that. Maybe because she'd had so few intimate relationships with men.

Wyatt had asked her about Patrick. She'd never thought of *him* that way. He'd always been too much like a brother to her.

In college, she'd had some relationships, but they'd been with guys who'd turned out to be looking for more of a bed partner than a life partner.

Or maybe that was her fault. Maybe she'd given off vibrations that had kept them from getting too close to her.

If you didn't feel good about your relationship with your father, could you feel good about your relationships with other men?

She'd never gotten that analytical about it. She'd just always known that it was hard for her to trust anyone with the intimate emotions she'd always kept to herself.

That didn't seem to be true with Wyatt Hawk. She wanted to feel close to him. But was she deliberately picking a guy she knew wouldn't let it happen?

She hated second-guessing herself. And him.

Was the danger swirling around them making her reach out toward him? Or was there something real developing between them—if both of them were willing to take the chance and let their guard down?

Chapter Six

Wyatt kept his gaze away from Carrie and forced his mind back to what he was supposed to be doing—figuring out who could be responsible for both the ambush and the kidnapping.

He walked to the table and picked up his computer, opening a web browser.

"You mentioned a Quincy Sumner?" he said.

"Yes."

"He lives in Fairfax?"

"Yes."

He put in the name and the Virginia city and came up with several hits right away. After scanning them quickly, he raised his head.

"It's not him."

"How do you know?"

"He's dead."

"He is?" she asked, surprise in her voice.

"Yeah. He had retired—then had a heart attack on the golf course a few months ago."

"Dad didn't mention it."

"Maybe he doesn't even know." Wyatt studied the

obituary, looking for names of next of kin. "I suppose it's possible that someone in his family could still hold a grudge against your father, but it seems unlikely that they'd be executing such an elaborate plan."

From the bed, Carrie murmured in agreement.

Wyatt bent his head to the computer screen again. "I've got some other ideas," he said as he scrolled through some of the files he'd stored in his mail system.

"Like what?"

"Let me check an address." He found the house he was searching for, then looked up. "I think the next step is to have a talk with Aaron Madison."

"Who is he?" Carrie asked.

"Another Federal prosecutor. He was working with Skip Gunderson."

"And you think he might know something?"

"He was in a position to know. This time you stay here, and keep the door locked." He closed the computer and stood up, thinking that going to Madison's house would get him away from Carrie for a while. And right now, he needed that distance. He'd done something stupid, and he didn't want to remain in the way of temptation.

But she apparently didn't understand his point of view—on any level.

"Uh, I don't think so."

He turned and faced her. "You don't think what?"

"I don't think you're leaving me here."

"It's the safest alternative."

Carrie stood and crossed the room, putting a firm hand on his arm.

He turned and looked at her. "Your father hired me to make judgment calls. It's safer if you stay here."

"Nothing's safe."

"But there's less risk keeping out of sight."

"That's not what you said before."

"The situation's changed."

"If you're going to talk to Madison, I'm going with you," she repeated. "I'm the one they're trying to kill, and I have the right to know what's going on."

He wanted to say they were trying to kill him, too. He wanted to add that she would be the next person to get any information he picked up, but he knew she wasn't going to accept that.

He sighed. "Okay." Walking over to the bag of clothing they'd bought, he pulled out black jeans and a black, long-sleeved polo shirt, which he took into the bathroom and put on.

When he came out, she gave him a curious look. "Are we going to talk to the man or break into his house?"

"You never know."

"Give me a minute."

She grabbed similar dark clothing and stepped into the bathroom. When she closed the door, he thought about leaving her in the motel but decided not to take the underhanded approach.

She came out a few moments later, and he handed her the hat and sunglasses he'd bought. "Put these on."

When she had complied, he studied her, trying to assess how much she looked like the woman he'd just seen on television. She'd lost weight since he'd met her, which made her face more angular.

"I can't wear the sunglasses after dark," she muttered.

"You'll wear them to the car now." He stopped and gave her a direct look. "And the same rules apply as when we were in the field outside the safe house. If I tell you to do something, you have to obey me."

"You mean like an S-and-M master?" she shot back.

He snorted. "You know what I mean."

"Yes."

"Then let me go out first."

"You wouldn't have tried to make me stay here if you thought it wasn't safe," she pointed out.

"Yeah, but I'm not taking any chances. When I give you the all clear, don't run to the car. Walk like we're here on a fun vacation."

"In Columbia?"

"Maybe you're planning a shopping trip to the Columbia Mall."

When she laughed, he said, "The point is, we don't want to attract any attention."

There were no problems on the way to the car. When Carrie had settled into her seat, he pulled out of the parking space. Twisting the wheel made his arm hurt, but he figured the pain would keep him focused. Beside him, Carrie took off the sunglasses, tucked them into her purse and folded her hands in her lap. She sat very still, and he wondered if she was thinking she shouldn't have come along.

Finally, she cleared her throat. "Tell me about Aaron Madison. Why do you think he could be a problem?"

"He certainly had access to the information about your trip downtown."

"Didn't a lot of government people?"

"Not really. They were trying to keep it under wraps so nothing bad would happen."

She made a dismissive sound. "Well, that certainly worked out well." After a few moments of silence, she asked, "What else about him made you wonder?"

"It's hard to say. There's something about him that I can't put into words. I guess you'd call it a hunch that he could be a problem. Maybe because he always seemed on edge when I talked with him."

"Meeting with me was a big responsibility. That could be why."

"Maybe," he said, but he was still wondering if it was something more sinister.

They rode in silence for a while before she asked, "Where does he live?"

"Bethesda," he answered, naming a close-in, expensive D.C. suburb.

"Won't his family wonder why we're dropping in after hours—or at all?"

"He doesn't have any children, and he and his wife, Rita, recently separated," he answered, glad to put the focus on Madison again.

"Do you know why?"

"No. I only know that she moved out a few months ago and got an apartment in one of the luxury buildings near the D.C. line."

"Isn't it unusual for the wife to be the one to leave?"

"Yes. That's one of the things I noticed."

"You had him investigated?"

"Not with any depth." He tightened his hands on the wheel. "Which may have been a mistake."

He waited for a comment on that, but she said nothing about his investigative skills. Instead, she said, "I met him briefly."

"How did he seem?"

She thought for a moment. "Anxious not to spend too much time with me. Now that I think back on it, I felt like he didn't want to get to know me very well."

Not a good sign, Wyatt thought as he drove down Route 29 to the Beltway, where he got off at the Connecticut Avenue exit, then took Bradley Boulevard, which was a shortcut to the section of the posh suburb where the Madison house was located.

Wyatt turned onto Wisconsin Avenue, then onto a side street where the houses were mostly brick two-stories that looked as though they had been built in the forties or fifties. Large trees marched up the green parkway between the curb and the sidewalk, and all the lawns and shrubbery were well maintained. It was obviously an upscale environment.

"A solid old neighborhood," Carrie remarked as she peered into the gathering darkness. "Which house is it?"

"157." He pointed to a redbrick colonial where most of the lights were turned off. When he got to the end of the block, he turned the corner, then did it again, putting them on the street in back of the Madison house.

"What are you doing?" Carrie asked.

"Taking precautions. I don't want anyone to know we're here."

"It would make for a quicker getaway if we parked closer."

"You think we'll need to get away fast?"

She shrugged. "I hope not. I guess I was thinking of what they do in action movies."

As they walked up the sidewalk and around the corner, Wyatt kept their pace moderate, as if they were out for an evening stroll. As far as he could see, there was no one else doing the same, and he hoped no one was looking out their windows trying to figure out who the man and woman were.

As they walked past parked cars, he looked inside but found them empty.

They reached 157 and turned into the driveway, which was about twenty-five yards long and sheltered by a tall hedge between Madison and the neighbors. At least that gave them a bit of privacy.

Carrie stared at the large two-story looming before them. "How can the guy afford all this on a government salary?"

Wyatt's thoughts were running along the same lines. "Maybe he inherited money. Or maybe he's got another source."

Wyatt walked softly up the blacktop driveway, trying to make as little noise as possible, listening for sounds from the house or the surroundings. There were none.

He got to a place where someone who pulled up in a car could turn off and take a path of wide stepping stones to the front door. Instead, he kept walking along the driveway. Carrie followed, and he was glad she wasn't asking questions.

They arrived at a six-foot-tall wooden fence to the backyard. The gate was standing open. Wyatt stepped through and looked around, then motioned for Carrie to follow. Inside the yard he led her toward the back door, which featured glass panes in the top half. Like the gate, it was standing ajar.

Beside him, she drew in a quick breath. "What's going on?" she whispered.

He shook his head, drawing his sidearm as he peered through the glass into the empty kitchen, where cabinets stood open and boxes of cereal and pasta had been thrown from the shelves onto the counters and the floor.

He cursed under his breath, wishing he'd insisted that Carrie stay at the motel. But she was here now, and he had to deal with it.

"Stay by the door," he whispered.

Entering the kitchen, he held his gun in a two-handed grip, swinging it in all directions, looking for whoever had made this mess. There appeared to be no one in this part of the house, but he took a quick run through the first-floor laundry room, then the living room and dining room before motioning Carrie to follow. Both rooms were in disarray, as though someone had conducted a search without caring how much mess they made.

"It's spooky." Carrie wrapped her arms around her shoulders. "What do you think happened?"

"Someone was searching—in a hurry."

"Are they gone?"

"It looks that way, unless they did the same thing we did and parked around the corner."

They walked quietly down a short hall toward the front of the house. On one side were double doors that led to a home office. Wyatt could see books pulled from the bookcase, the rug turned up, credenza drawers open. There was also a glass and a bottle of Jack Daniel's spilled on the rug.

It was a worse mess than in the kitchen, but there was something even more disturbing—a pair of men's shoes and trouser-clad legs sticking out from one side of the desk.

Carrie gasped.

"Stay back."

Wyatt rushed forward and found the man he'd been looking for lying on the floor behind the desk.

Aaron Madison was in his early forties with a receding hairline. Once, his features had been handsome. Now his face was battered, and his glasses lay on the floor near the wall, shattered. His eyes were closed, but one was badly swollen. His nose was smashed, and his lips were split and bloody. His shirt was open, and Wyatt saw that a knife had been used to carve up his chest, but not so deeply that he was going to die right away.

He'd hoped to spare Carrie the gruesome sight, but he knew she was right behind him.

"Oh, Lord," she gasped as she stared at the man. "Who did this to him?"

"I hope it's not someone trying to get information about you."

When she sucked in a sharp breath, he wished he'd kept that thought to himself. As he knelt beside Madison, he pressed two fingers to the man's neck, where he felt a faint pulse.

"He's alive." Barely, he thought. "Someone worked him over. The same someone who trashed the house. I'm going to call an ambulance."

The man's good eye fluttered open and focused on Wyatt. "Too late," he whispered. "Internal injuries…bad."

"Who did this?"

Instead of answering, Madison asked, "Wyatt Hawk? What…are you doing…here?"

"A hunch. Who did this?"

Again Madison ignored the question as though it were dangerous to tell what had happened to him. Even now.

"They didn't get into the safe," Madison whispered. He dragged in a rattling breath.

"You need—"

"To tell you the combo…twenty-six right." He paused. "Fifteen left." Again he stopped to catch his breath. "Double right turn to seventy-two."

After delivering the message, he closed his eyes again. Wyatt gripped his shoulder. "Where is the safe?"

"Behind…medicine cabinet in bathroom down the hall."

"Stay with him," Wyatt said to Carrie. "See if he can tell you anything else."

Carrie knelt beside the man. "You need medical attention," she murmured.

Wyatt left the gun with Carrie and hurried down the hall to the bathroom. The medicine cabinet stood open, and the contents were scattered around the small room, but the cabinet itself was undisturbed. It was not a standard model but an ornately carved wooden box that was fixed to the wall with hooks above the top pediment. The bottom rested on a bracket.

Wyatt lifted the cabinet up, detaching it and setting it on the floor, revealing a safe embedded in the wall. Quickly he began spinning the dial, working the combination that Madison had given him.

Twenty-six right, fifteen left. Double right turn to seventy-two. With the last turn, the lock clicked, and he pulled the door open. There was a wad of folded bills inside—ranging from twenties to hundreds. Beside them was a small notebook. Wyatt left the money and took out the book, thumbing through the pages. There were number notations, but he couldn't tell what they meant, exactly. He'd have to ask Madison.

A noise behind him made him whirl. It was Carrie, her face stark.

"I guess he didn't make it?"

"No," she choked out.

"Did he say anything?"

"He looked at me and said he'd been stupid."

"That's all?"

"Yes."

"Did he know who you were?"

"I think so." She swallowed hard. "He must have betrayed me, and—"

"Don't jump to conclusions."

"It has to do with me!"

"But maybe not the way you think." Wyatt held up the book. "We don't know how he's connected to the ambush, if he is at all, but I think this is what the people who searched the house were looking for."

"Lucky we didn't run into them."

He nodded and handed the book to her, watching as she flipped through the pages. "What is it?"

She shook her head. "No idea."

As they stood in the bathroom, he became aware of a background noise that grew and swelled—a siren coming closer. "The cops are coming," he muttered. "We'd better split."

"What about Madison?"

"We can't do anything for him."

He reached for a tissue from the box on top of the toilet tank and wiped his fingerprints off the safe dial. Had he touched anything in the office where the cops could get prints? He hoped not.

The siren was getting louder. "Come on."

He sprinted back down the hall and grabbed the gun she'd left on the floor.

"Sorry," she muttered.

"Not your job."

He led her into the kitchen and out the door. On the street, he could see flashing red and blue lights. They couldn't get out that way, but could they get out at all?

Silently cursing the bad timing, he led her into the backyard, around a swimming pool and over to the back fence, which was about six feet tall. Too bad Madison had been so conscientious about enclosing the pool.

When he saw Carrie eyeing the fence, he said, "Let me go first."

He hoisted himself up and scrambled over. On

the other side there were rails where he could rest his feet. Reaching down, he grabbed Carrie's hand, helping her up and over. They both dropped to the ground in the yard behind Madison's.

From the other side of the fence, they heard running feet in the driveway, but now they were screened from view.

"Come on."

Thankful that he'd followed his instincts and parked on the opposite street, Wyatt started across the yard in back of the Madison house, another suburban oasis, also featuring a pool.

Before he and Carrie had made it halfway, a dog began to bark, and he cursed again. It sounded medium-size, and maybe the cops would think the animal was barking at *them*.

Apparently, the canine was in the house. Hoping the owner wasn't going to let it out, he kept moving through the yard.

Lights were already flicking on in the house, and he ducked low as he reached the neighbor's gate and swung it open.

They hurried through, and he thought they were going to make it to the street without further incident when floodlights clicked on, illuminating the yard.

Grabbing Carrie, Wyatt threw them both into the shrubbery moments before a door opened.

He waited with his heart pounding, peering out and seeing a man dressed in jeans and a button-down shirt standing in the light coming from the front hall.

Wyatt had a gun and the homeowner probably didn't, but he wasn't going to shoot anybody.

Beside him he could feel Carrie waiting tensely and put a reassuring hand on her arm.

Seconds ticked by. Praying that the guy wasn't stupid enough to put himself in danger, Wyatt forced himself to wait. Finally he heard the front door shut again. He stayed where he was for another minute, but he knew that the cops could come this way any moment.

"Got to move," he whispered. "Stay in the bushes."

They crawled through the shrubbery to the next house and waited again.

When he heard more footsteps, he tensed. This time it was a patrol officer, coming along the sidewalk, shining his light into the greenery.

Chapter Seven

Wyatt pressed Carrie down, flattening himself on top of her, hiding his face and hoping that their dark clothing would keep them from being discovered.

With his mouth near her ear, he whispered, "Don't look up."

Tension zinged through him as the cop made his slow way up the sidewalk.

When Wyatt heard the footsteps stop, every muscle in his body tightened as he ran scenarios through his mind.

They were on the run from terrorists, and maybe he could explain why they'd decided to question Aaron Madison, but he knew that if the cops found them, they'd be in for a long interrogation—which would put Carrie in danger because there was no way of knowing who was feeding information to the bad guys.

Hoping he wasn't going to have to assault the officer, he waited with his muscles coiled. Below him he could almost feel Carrie vibrating with nerves.

When the footsteps moved on, he and Carrie both

stayed where they were. Finally he lifted his head, slid off of Carrie's body and crawled far enough forward so that he could see out. The street and sidewalk were clear.

"I'm going to get the car," he said. "You stay here."

He braced for her objection, but she must have remembered his caution about following his directions.

"I have to keep low, so it might take some time," he whispered.

"Okay."

"Watch out for me. I'll drive up the block with my lights off."

Again she murmured her assent.

He stayed low to the ground, wishing he could move faster. It was hard going, especially with his wounded arm throbbing. After passing three houses, he decided to take a chance on standing.

Fighting the impulse to run, he walked the rest of the way to the car, then climbed in and shut the door quickly to kill the light. He threw the switch, so the light wouldn't turn on when he opened the door again, and started the engine, then drove at a normal pace toward the house where he'd left Carrie.

When he eased to the curb, she emerged from the bushes and raced toward the car.

Once she was inside, he turned on his headlights so he wouldn't look suspicious and pulled away before she'd buckled her seat belt.

As they rounded the corner on the perpendicular

street, he could see several pairs of flashing lights in front of the dead man's house.

He turned the other way, still driving like a responsible citizen as he made his way back toward Wisconsin Avenue.

"Will they know we were there?" Carrie asked.

"I don't know. Depends on if we left prints. Or if someone spotted us and reported they saw a man and a woman go into the house."

"That doesn't prove it was us."

"No. But they might make assumptions."

She picked up Madison's book from where Wyatt had stuffed it between the seats, switched on the reading light and thumbed through the pages. "I'd like to know what this signifies. Some numbers have a plus in front of them and some have a minus."

"And there are dates?"

"Yes. I guess that meant something to him."

She turned to the last few pages. "In this part, it seems to be all minuses. Wait, here's a plus."

"What's the number?"

"Twenty thousand."

"Interesting. What are the minus numbers?"

"Smaller. Five thousand. Three thousand. Two thousand." Carrie sighed.

"Do the dates start before you saw the terrorists in the park?"

"Yes."

"So it might not be related. Let's put the book on hold and see if the murder made the news yet."

She switched off the reading light, turned on the radio and found the all-news station. They sat through some sports scores, political news and ads before an announcer said, "Police are investigating the murder of a U.S. Attorney at his home in Bethesda, Maryland, this evening. Aaron Madison had been severely beaten before his death. Two people—Carrie Mitchell and Wyatt Hawk—are wanted for questioning in conjunction with the murder."

Carrie gasped. "What?"

Wyatt put a hand on her arm. "Quiet. I want to hear the rest of it."

The newsreader was saying, "Earlier today, Mitchell was supposed to meet with a U.S. Attorney in connection with a terrorist plot she allegedly overheard. That official, Skip Gunderson, was also found dead in the offices where he was scheduled to meet Mitchell. She and Wyatt Hawk have been missing since the morning incident."

Carrie turned to him, her face suffused with panic. "It's too quick for fingerprints."

He worked to keep his voice steady. "Like I said, somebody could have seen us sneaking around. It could be the person who called the cops." Wyatt clenched his hands on the wheel. "But how did they know my name? That was never made public." He turned toward her. "We're back to the set of people who knew your father hired me."

"If the cops catch us…"

He swallowed, then told her what he'd been thinking but hadn't wanted to say before. "They can hold us on national-security grounds."

"Why?"

"Because this all started with a terrorist plot."

"You're talking about them holding us forever without a lawyer?"

"Right."

"But I'm the one who turned the terrorists in."

"And now a lot of people are dead, and nobody can be sure of your motives."

They rode in silence for a while. Up the road Wyatt saw flashing red and blue lights.

"Oh, Lord. A cop car," Carrie breathed. "Is he after us?"

"If he were, he wouldn't just be sitting there," Wyatt answered, hoping he had assessed the situation correctly. Still, he started looking for a place to turn off and saw none.

Beside him, Carrie had clenched her fingers together in her lap. He reached out and laid a hand on her arm.

"It's probably a traffic stop."

She didn't answer, but when they got close enough he saw that he was right, and they drove by without the cop leaping into the road and pointing a gun at them.

Beside him, Carrie whispered, "I hate to clench up every time we see a motorist pulled over."

"The police don't know about this car. Nobody

saw it near Madison's house, and I rented it under a different name."

She nodded.

"And we're going to stay under the radar. But first…"

When he pulled into the parking lot of a small grocery store, she looked up. "What?"

"We can get a few things to eat. What do you want?"

"Surprise me," she said without much enthusiasm.

"Slide down in the seat while I'm gone."

She did as he'd asked, and he made a quick trip through the store, getting some premade deli sandwiches, drinks and snacks.

When he returned to the car, he found her watching for him but didn't bother to remind her that she'd been supposed to stay down.

They made it back to the motel, where Wyatt drove around the parking lot a couple of times before finding a spot near their door. He had Carrie wait while he checked the room, then motioned for her to follow. She came inside and leaned against the closed door.

"I hate this," she murmured as she picked up the remote and pointed it at the television. She caught an account of the information they'd already heard— along with something new. This time there was a picture of Wyatt, taken when he was still with the CIA.

He muttered a curse.

Carrie stared at the picture. "I guess it's not recent."

"Thank God for small favors."

He put the milk and juice he'd bought into the small refrigerator.

"Want a drink?"

"Are you offering me liquor?"

"No. Maybe orange juice or soda water."

"Juice."

He poured them both a drink and watched her trying to relax as she took small sips.

He wanted to put his arms around her, but he knew it was a lot more prudent to keep his hands off of her. Too bad they couldn't get some distance from each other. But he couldn't let her stay in a separate room now—not even a suite. He wanted her where he could see her—except when she was in the bathroom.

"Watch a movie," he said.

"I won't be able to concentrate."

"It's a better choice than worrying."

She kicked off her shoes, pulled down the spread, then got up and opened one of the bags from the discount department store, which she took into the bathroom. He heard the toilet flush, then water running in the shower, and he remembered that they'd spent part of the evening lying in the dirt. She was in the shower for a long time. When she emerged from the bathroom, she'd changed into a clean shirt and pair of jeans. Probably the way to go, he decided.

"Feel better?" he asked.

"Yes. A shower always helps."

She brought over one of the sandwiches and unwrapped it, then started flipping channels. He didn't want to watch the television, and he didn't want to watch her.

Instead, he took a quick shower, keeping his wounded arm out of the water, and changed, then took the other sandwich to the table, where he ate and studied the book he had taken from Madison's house.

Suppose the notations were for money either received or owed on a given date? What would that mean? Was he involved in some business—possibly an illegal enterprise, which he conducted on a cash-only basis? Suppose he'd been keeping the information from his wife, and she'd found out and left him?

Perhaps Rita Madison could solve the mystery of the notations. The next logical step would be to visit her, if they could do it without attracting attention.

He glanced over at Carrie and saw that she had slumped down on the bed, and was now asleep.

He called her name softly, but she didn't answer. He found the remote where she'd laid it and clicked off the television, killing the background noise in the room. Then he took the remains of the sandwich off the bed and threw it away.

Carrie was lying on top of the covers. He figured he should wake her so she could get properly into the bed. Then he decided that it would be better to simply let her sleep because she had had a hell of a day, and he knew she needed to rest.

Which created a problem. He could try to stay awake to keep guard, but he'd had the same horrible day—worse, if you factored in getting shot. If he didn't get some sleep, he was going to be in bad shape tomorrow, when he'd need his wits about him to figure out what the hell was going on.

He walked to her bed, looking down at her for a few minutes and listening to her even breathing.

At the safe house, he'd tried to avoid direct contact with her, but he'd studied her covertly. Now he allowed himself the pleasure of taking in her delicate features, the long lashes fanning her cheeks, the short, dark hair that certainly wasn't her natural look but worked, because she'd be beautiful with any hairstyle or color.

He drank his fill of her face, then let his eyes travel downward, pausing at the creamy hollow at the base of her throat, the swell of her breasts, the curve of her hips. He imagined himself climbing into bed with her, taking her in his arms, caressing all the sweet places he longed to touch. When he found himself getting hard, he turned away and grabbed the bag of supplies she'd bought at the drugstore as well as one of the bags from the department store.

After quietly closing the bathroom door, he took off his shirt and then the bandage. His arm hurt when he flexed it, but there was only a little blood on the gauze pads he'd removed. Turning so that he could study the wound in the mirror, he saw that it looked as if it was healing okay. He poked at the margins, finding them tender but not swollen. After applying more antiseptic, he redressed the wound.

When he exited the bathroom, he left the light on and the door ajar. Looking at the clock on the table between the beds, he saw that it was after eleven. He wasn't expecting trouble, but sleeping in his clothes wasn't a bad idea.

He kicked off his shoes and turned down the spread on his bed. He kept himself awake for an hour researching Aaron Madison on the web. Finally, when his eyes became heavy-lidded, he eased down on the bed and reviewed everything that had happened in the past fifteen hours. It seemed like too much for one day. But he knew that it had all been real.

He closed his eyes, knowing that any hint of danger would bring him awake.

CARRIE WAS TOTALLY unaware of her surroundings. At first she slept soundly, the events of the day acting like a drug to wipe out her consciousness. The blissful peace lasted for a few hours. Then from one moment to the next, she was plunged into a dream. A dream that made her gasp. She struggled to pull away, but it held her fast, its grip like a choke hold around her neck.

A silent scream rose in her throat, but it never

reached her lips as she fought against the terror of the dream.

She knew at once what was coming, a repeat of her day, only this time the colors were somber, and ominous music was playing in the background, as though she was watching another television program. But this time she wasn't a spectator. She was in the middle of it, and she knew from the music that something bad was going to happen.

Suddenly she was in the backseat of the big black car on the way to meet Skip Gunderson, the Federal prosecutor. It was her duty. She'd known that all along, but as she sat next to Wyatt, tension vibrated through her. She was waiting for the worst, because this time she knew what was going to happen. She was back where she had been with Wyatt at the beginning. He'd been cold and distant. Now he sat like a statue, his gaze fixed in the distance.

"Wyatt?"

He didn't answer, didn't even turn his head toward her. She wanted to reach out and grab him, but she knew it wouldn't do her any good.

Her nerves pulled taut as a rubber band about to snap when the car stopped at the barrier outside the garage. Even knowing what was coming, she couldn't make herself leap away. The fake guard thrust his arm into the car and shot at them, just as he had that morning, and Wyatt finally moved, shooting the man before pulling her out of the car.

She relived her flight with Wyatt into the building.

Only this time it was different. This time she was sure they would never get away. Wyatt was running through endless brightly lit corridors, with terrorists leaping out of doorways and shooting, the bullets smashing into the hallway floors just behind them. It was all so real and vivid that she knew she and Wyatt were going to die.

She moaned, struggling to fight her way out of the awful nightmare, her head thrashing back and forth. When she felt arms restraining her, she cried out and tried to wrench away, sure that one of the terrorists had grabbed her and was holding fast.

She struggled against him, kicking out with her feet and slamming her hands into him, hearing him grunt in pain.

He was speaking, and she tried to focus on the words.

"Carrie. It's okay. Carrie, it's Wyatt."

"Wyatt?"

Her eyes blinked open, staring up into his face.

"Wyatt?" she said again.

"Yes."

She dragged in a breath and let it out as she realized she'd been kicking and hitting him.

"I hurt you. Oh, Lord, I'm so sorry."

"I'm okay."

She knew it was Wyatt above her. She wasn't sure of much else. She wasn't in her condo in D.C. Or at her father's estate. She wasn't at the safe house. But she was lying in bed with her clothes on.

Then reality slammed back into her. The night-mare was a replay of reality. Her new reality.

"You were having a bad dream," he murmured.

"Yes. And you were so distant…like you were at first, and I hated that."

The moment the words were out of her mouth, she wished she could take them back.

"I'm sorry."

"It wasn't your fault. It was my subconscious." She winced, wondering if that sounded any better.

A shaft of illumination came from the bathroom. Because she needed to look away from him, she swung her head toward the clock, but she was lying at the wrong angle to see it.

"What time is it?"

"Four in the morning."

"I woke you up." And she'd given away the fear she'd tried to suppress, but it had invaded her sleep. She wasn't sure which was worse.

"It's okay. Do you want to talk about it?"

Not really, she thought. But she owed him an explanation.

"It was what happened this morning. You took me down to the Federal office building. You shot that fake security guard. Then the terrorists were chasing us through the building. We were running down corridors, and they were always behind us—shooting."

He had been looming over her. Now he eased down beside her, stroking her arm, then her hair. "That must have been terrifying."

"I was sure we wouldn't get away."

She rolled toward him, seeking the warmth of his body. She didn't want to think about the dream, and she didn't want to talk about it anymore.

"It's all right, sweetheart," he murmured, his mouth close to her ear.

Sweetheart. Had the endearment somehow slipped out because he was trying to reassure her? Or had he meant it? And was there a way to find out?

Overcome with emotions, she turned her head, so that her lips brushed his mouth.

When she sensed that he might draw away, she cupped her hand around the back of his head to hold him where he was. This morning the idea of kissing Wyatt would never have entered her mind. He'd been too distant and unapproachable. Now she knew that he'd wanted her to see him that way because he'd been trying to keep their relationship strictly professional.

Since this morning she'd learned to see him differently. And she'd learned something about herself, too. In her life she'd made sure she needed nobody besides herself. Now she needed this man in ways she couldn't even understand.

Their lips held, and she clung to him, because her world—the world where she had lived all her life—had come crashing down around her head, and Wyatt Hawk was the only point of stability in a universe that had turned itself upside down.

If he drew back now, reality would crumble.

When his lips pressed more firmly to hers, she returned the kiss. She knew she wanted comfort from him, but she wanted—needed—so much more. And she knew in that moment that he needed the same things she did, knew it from the way he began to feast on her, with hunger and passion and perhaps the edge of desperation.

They'd been through hell today. And they had only each other.

Her heart started to beat faster, and faster still when he gathered her closer and his hands moved restlessly across her back. His touch had begun as comforting; now it spoke of a sensuality she hadn't dared to hope he possessed.

Or perhaps she had known and sensed that he had buried it deep inside himself. And she had brought it to the surface.

That knowledge made her heart leap.

It was a potent combination. The man who had signed on to protect her and had proved his worth a thousand times over. And the man who had proved he cared more about her than himself.

For long moments he stroked her, caressing her breasts, her hips, her bottom, sending ripples of sensation over her skin, sensations that sank into her body, heating her from the inside out. How could she ever have thought him cold? His mere touch took her breath away.

As she felt the heat build between them, she closed her eyes, clinging to him, rocking with him on the bed. When she felt his erection pressing against her middle, she knew without a doubt where they were headed, and she rejoiced in the knowledge—until the moment when she felt him pull away.

Her eyes blinked open and stared into the dark depths of his. "Wyatt?"

His voice had turned gritty. "You know we can't do this."

"Why not?" she asked, somehow managing to keep her voice even. "We both want—"

He pressed his fingers against her lips, preventing her from finishing the sentence. "Wanting isn't the issue. We've both been through an emotional roller coaster today. You're reacting to the dream and to almost getting killed. I'm…"

This time he was the one who stopped.

"You're what?"

"Taking advantage of you."

"No."

He might be putting it that way, but she knew it wasn't the truth. He wasn't taking any more than he was giving.

"You're in a fragile emotional state," he added.

She swallowed. He could be speaking the truth as he knew it, but she didn't want to hear his assessment of the heat that had flared between them.

He sat up and ran a hand through his dark hair. Then he moved to the side of the bed and got up, putting several feet of space between them as he stood there breathing hard.

She was also struggling to control her breathing, and listening to the wild pounding of her heart.

She wondered what would happen if she got off the bed and reached for him. Would he come back and take up where they'd left off?

It was tempting to try it, but she didn't want a second rejection.

Instead, she got up and pulled the covers aside so that she could climb in.

"Are you going to be okay?" he asked.

She might have told him she wanted to be held. Instead, she said, "Yes," and fixed the pillow more comfortably under her neck as she closed her eyes.

She could feel him watching her for a few more moments. She thought he'd get back into bed. Instead, as she watched through slitted lids, he walked to the table where he'd left his computer and sat down, leaning toward the screen as he accessed material she couldn't see.

She kept covertly watching him, sure she wouldn't get back to sleep. But finally she surrendered to fatigue. The next time she opened her eyes, she smelled coffee.

Blinking, she looked at Wyatt, then at the clock. It was after nine.

"Why didn't you wake me up?"

"You needed the sleep. They have breakfast here. I got us both something. Better than last night's stale sandwiches." He kept his voice matter-of-fact, as though nothing personal had happened between them in the night.

If he could do it, so could she. "Thanks."

He set down a cardboard tray with coffee, juice, cinnamon buns and hard-boiled eggs. She joined him at the table, and they both drank coffee and ate.

"What were you working on when I fell asleep?" she asked as she glanced toward his computer.

"A couple of things. I got the address of Madison's wife, but I'm afraid that if we go over there, we're going to run into a bunch of people."

"If we get some dressier clothing, we can go in as friends of her husband, then ask to speak to her privately."

"That might work. But it could be dangerous."

Setting down her coffee cup, she picked up the remote control and turned to CNN. She and Wyatt were still of interest, starting with a rehash of the attack at the Federal Building and progressing to speculation about whether they had been at Aaron Madison's house.

"His poor wife," Carrie murmured. "Even if they were having problems, his death has to be a shock."

DOUGLAS MITCHELL MOVED restlessly on the narrow bed. His captors had let him get up to go to the bathroom. Then they had secured his hand to the bed again. And they'd given him a bottle of water and a sandwich. Something from a deli, he judged.

He sat in the dark, eating the food slowly and drinking the water.

He wasn't sure how long the men had been holding him. He shook his head. Sometimes it felt as if he'd been here for hours, sometimes days, and the sense of time distortion was maddening.

One thing he did know: Carrie must still be on the loose. These men hadn't captured or killed her because he was still alive.

He clenched his teeth together, hating that he was at the mercy of these men.

He'd seen three of them when they'd let him out for his bathroom break. They were all young. In their late twenties and early thirties, he judged.

And they all looked like American men from the Midwest. Not what he'd consider typical terrorists.

Well, maybe they were, if you thought about Timothy McVeigh. But McVeigh had been a fanatic. These guys had talked about getting money for what they were doing. Did that mean they didn't care about their terrorist plot?

He took another swallow of the water. Should he drink it all or save some for later?

Maybe saving it was best. But maybe he should eat more of the sandwich. It wouldn't keep, would it?

It was still hard to think about what to do, but it felt as though his mind wasn't quite as fuzzy as it had been.

Did he recognize this house? He wasn't sure, but he thought it looked familiar.

He remembered a friend talking about his own mind being fuzzy. The guy had been on a gazillion medications, and he was having problems with his memory. Then his doctor had cut back some of his meds, and he'd started thinking better.

Could that be his problem?

Chapter Eight

Wyatt gave Carrie a direct look. "I have to think Madison's involved."

"It could be a coincidence," she argued.

"You mean his house getting searched and his getting killed the same day you're supposed to meet Gunderson and someone tries to kill you? Highly unlikely."

"Then we should go with the paying-our-respects-to-the-widow plan."

"And if there's a TV truck outside, we drive past."

"And then what?"

"Go on to the next best lead."

"Which is?"

"I'm thinking."

When Carrie finished her breakfast, she took the toiletries she'd bought into the bathroom and got dressed.

"We're going to have to stop at a more upscale department store," he said as he eyed her jeans and T-shirt.

She nodded.

"I wish we didn't have to go out in public."

"I'll be quick," she answered, starting to mentally plan what she could buy. If she got a dress, she'd also have to buy stockings and good shoes. Probably it was better to stick to dress slacks and a dark jacket.

"Are we checking out?" she asked, as he gathered up his belongings.

"Probably better not to stay in the same place for two nights."

"Then we should get suitcases, too."

She gathered up the things she'd bought and put them back into the bags.

"Put on your hat," Wyatt said.

"I actually hate hats."

"When this is over, you'll never have to wear one again."

And would he be around to see her with the dye out of her hair and the length back? Did she want him to be?

The answer was yes, but she couldn't focus on that. Right now she had to make sure there was life after hiding out.

He repeated the security procedures from the night before, then motioned her to the car.

They drove to the Columbia Mall.

"Macy's is probably the best bet," she said.

"Okay. I'll get slacks, a dress shirt, a sports jacket and loafers, then meet you in the luggage department. And one more thing. The store probably has security cameras, and there will be cameras outside the building where Mrs. Madison lives. Keep your gaze down, like you need to watch your feet to walk straight."

"You think the police will be looking at cameras here?"

"Like I said, it's always better to be prepared. If somebody thinks they've spotted us, the cops might go back over the security tapes."

Inside they split up.

Carrie had never liked clothes shopping. And she liked it even less this morning because she kept wondering if anyone was watching her. To minimize her exposure, she tried to streamline the process. First she picked up slacks she thought would fit. Then she found a black blazer with narrow white stripes and paired it with a simple white knit top. Her selections fit and didn't look too bad with the low shoes she'd worn to the meeting with Gunderson that never happened. She took the tags off the new clothing and brought them to the checkout counter, then asked the clerk to put what she'd been wearing in the store bag.

At the luggage department, she didn't spot Wyatt at first. Then a tall man in a navy sports jacket and gray pants turned around, and she realized she'd been totally faked out. She'd seen him in only casual clothing, looking like a rough-around-the-edges secret agent. But he was very polished in the dressier outfit, as if he could fit right into a boardroom.

"You clean up pretty well," she murmured.

"You do, too," he answered, eyeing her conservative yet flattering outfit.

He paid for the luggage, and they went back to the car. After stowing the department-store bags in the one of the suitcases, they headed back the way they'd come the day before, taking the same route to the Beltway and then to Wisconsin Avenue.

"We should plan how we're going to represent ourselves to various people," Wyatt said.

"Okay. How do you want to play it?"

"I think that if anyone else is with Rita—or asks how we know Aaron—we say we're friends from the country club."

"Which club?"

He named a well-known club off of Connecticut Avenue in Chevy Chase.

"What if people who really knew him there are around?"

"Unlikely. They kicked him out six months ago when he couldn't pay the membership fees."

"And you know all that how?"

"I researched him on the web after you went to sleep. Then I did some more poking around in the morning."

"What else did you find out?"

"That his credit cards were maxed out. I also know that his wife has a trust fund from her family. She used it to buy her apartment."

"So she wasn't dependent on her husband."

"Right. Which is lucky for her."

"Describe her to me, so I don't start talking to another guest like she's the widow."

"She's a good-looking blonde woman in her late thirties. Her hair is in a short pageboy. Her makeup is always impeccable. She's the kind who takes good care of herself and wouldn't allow an ounce of extra fat to spoil the look of her size-four figure."

"It sounds like you don't approve of slender women."

He gave her a quick look, then glanced back at the road. "I don't like this obsession in our society with trying to look model thin."

"There are a lot of people who are overweight."

"Yeah. A weird contrast."

They drove in silence for another few minutes before Wyatt cleared his throat.

"Yes?" she asked.

"About our cover story… Maybe we should pretend to be a married couple."

After he dropped the comment, silence hung between them for a few seconds. Carrie could imagine he hadn't liked making the suggestion, and she couldn't stop herself from needling him.

"Why, exactly?"

"Because that's the easiest explanation of why we're showing up together. Do you have a better idea?"

"We both worked downtown with him."

"Rita probably met the office staff," he shot back.

"Right. I guess we have to use the country-club story—and false names, too."

"Since I'm already Will Hanks," he said, using the alias he'd used at the rental-car place and the motel, "you can be Carolyn Hanks."

"You came up with that fast. Were you already thinking about my name?"

He nodded.

"Carolyn Hanks and Will Hanks," she said, trying out the names. "If we get a chance to talk to Rita, maybe I should be the one who starts the conversation."

"Why?"

"Because it will be woman to woman, and she may say things to me that she wouldn't say to you."

He thought for a moment. "Okay, that makes sense, but maybe we need to have a legend planned so we don't get caught in any traps."

"What's a legend?"

"A spy's cover story. What if you lost your first husband a few years ago, and you have some idea of how she feels."

"We're getting into an elaborate scenario, don't you think?"

"We need to be prepared."

"Then what did you do with Aaron at the country club? Golf? Tennis? Do we know what he did there?"

He made a dismissive sound. "I can't fake my way through golf or tennis. Let's say we met in the weight room."

"Okay," she answered, remembering that Wyatt had been a faithful user of the weights at the safe house. The memory stopped her for a moment. Living with him and using the weight room had been part of her routine for a week. Now that seemed like another life. In fact, her whole world had been turned upside down and righted again—with yet a different view of reality each time.

They arrived at Rita Madison's apartment building, which was one of the expensive high-rises near the upscale shopping complex at Wisconsin and Western. They drove by, checking out the environment.

"No TV trucks," Carrie said.

"Let's hope reporters aren't hiding in the bushes."

She gave him a sharp look. "Do you think they would?"

"You never know what they're going to do. Like I said, I'm wondering how they got my photo."

The comment set Carrie's teeth on edge, and she kept her guard up as they walked back toward the building and stepped into the lobby. Apparently, it was the kind of place where you didn't get past the first floor unless you lived there—or were announced.

"May I help you?" asked an older woman in a dark suit who was standing behind a counter resembling a hotel check-in desk.

Wyatt approached her, and Carrie followed.

"We're here to pay our respects to Rita Madison, apartment three fifteen."

The woman pulled a long face. "Yes, it's so sad. We heard it on the news last night. Mrs. Madison only moved in a few months ago."

"After she separated from Aaron?" Wyatt asked.

"Yes."

"We were hoping they'd get back together," Wyatt said, as though he was an old friend of both of theirs.

Still, he broke off the conversation before it went any further.

When the elevator door had closed behind them, he said, "We don't want to call too much attention to ourselves."

She nodded, thinking that he should have been an actor. He was good at slipping into a persona. Like he'd done with her. At first at the safe house, she'd thought he was cold and distant because that was what he'd wanted her to think. Then she'd known it was a pose. And what about his relationship with her now? Was there any way to know what he was really thinking?

She stopped trying to puzzle it out as they reached the third floor and the elevator doors opened.

As they walked down the hall, she saw that the door to number 315 was ajar, probably so that Mrs. Madison didn't have to keep getting up to let visitors in.

They walked into a marble-floored vestibule that could have been the front entryway to a good-size house. Beyond was a living room with very formal furniture—reproductions of seventeenth-century English pieces, Carrie judged.

She spotted Rita Madison right away. She saw the blond hair and the slender form, although the woman had not taken the care with her makeup that Wyatt had described. She was speaking to a man in a black suit wearing a black shirt with a white collar. Her minister. Other people stood around the room. Some were talking quietly while others were drinking coffee or eating from small plates of food.

Carrie looked toward the dining table and saw that various buffet items had been set out. A young, dark-haired woman in a black uniform stepped into the room and began collecting dirty plates and glasses. It was a pretty good spread for having been organized at short notice.

Rita Madison must have been keeping one eye on the door. She glanced up, spotted them and stiffened. For a moment, Carrie thought she had recognized them from the news reports of the murder. Or could the police have shown her pictures of them?

Then she told herself that the woman was probably only wondering who these people were that she didn't know. Was Rita worried about her husband's associates? Did she think some of them might show up and cause trouble?

Carrie hated having to speculate on every small thing that happened. It would be great to have her nice, normal life back. Or would it? That life hadn't included Wyatt Hawk. When this was over, she could imagine that he'd walk away from her—because he thought it was the right thing to do. Never mind what she thought.

She struggled to put those particular speculations aside as she crossed the room with Wyatt at her side.

"Mrs. Madison?" Carrie said. "I'm sorry to be meeting you under such sad circumstances, but we wanted to stop by and pay our respects."

The minister touched her shoulder. "I'll just go and get some coffee and leave you to greet your guests."

It looked as if Rita wasn't sure she wanted the man to leave her side. But she didn't stop him from heading into the dining room, where he started filling a plate at the buffet table.

The widow turned to Carrie. Her voice was cool as she asked, "Who are you?"

Wyatt answered. "We know…or rather I knew Aaron from the club. He and I used to get into conversations in the weight room. We had a little competition going about how much we could bench-press."

"Yes, Aaron was very competitive," Rita murmured.

"I'm Will Hanks. And this is my wife, Carolyn," Wyatt said.

"Nice to meet you." She stopped and sighed. "I guess that's not the right way to put it. I'm not sure what the right way is."

"I know," Carrie said sympathetically. "I lost my

first husband a few years ago, so I know what you're going through."

Rita nodded.

"I'm wondering if we could speak in private," Wyatt said.

"About what?"

"Something Aaron wouldn't want us discussing in front of a bunch of people."

The words must have raised alarm bells, because she gave Wyatt and Carrie a penetrating look.

"Could we please talk privately?" Carrie said again. "It's important."

The woman hesitated, glancing around the room. Lowering her voice, she said, "I guess you're not going to murder me if we step into the bedroom."

"Hardly," Wyatt answered.

She turned and walked quickly down the hall, and they followed.

Carrie gave Wyatt a look that said, *Easier than I expected.*

He gave her a cautious look in return.

They reached a large bedroom, decorated in similar style to the rest of the apartment.

Once inside, Rita closed the door, then crossed to the bedside table and bent down to open a drawer. When she turned to face them again, she was holding a small revolver in a hand that wasn't quite steady.

Carrie choked back a gasp. Beside her she could feel the tension radiating through Wyatt's body.

"You're lying about how you knew Aaron. I think

you'd better tell me what's going on," the widow said in a hard voice. "Or maybe tell me why I shouldn't call 911."

Carrie's heart leaped into her throat as she looked from the gun to the angry eyes confronting her. As she struggled to speak, Wyatt said, "We came to you because we're in trouble, and we hope you can help us."

"You're the couple the police are looking for, aren't you?"

"Yes."

"Did you kill my husband?"

"No."

"But you were at his house last night. And everything you've said about your background is a lie. You didn't know Aaron."

"I met him because he was involved in Carrie's case," Wyatt said. "I'm sorry we made up a story, but we needed a reason to walk into your home, because we need to ask you some questions."

"What do you know about my husband's death?"

"When we arrived at the house he was lying on the floor, bleeding," Wyatt answered. "There was nothing we could do for him."

Rita made a moaning sound. "If I'd been there…"

"They probably would have killed you, too," Wyatt said.

Carrie watched a shudder go through the woman.

To Carrie's relief, she lowered the gun. But she didn't put it down. "Tell me what you found."

"The house had been searched by someone who didn't care about making a mess. Aaron was in his office. He was struggling to give us information—before it was too late. He gave me the combination to his safe."

Mrs. Madison's eyes widened. "His safe."

"Did you know what was in it?"

"Aaron never gave me the combination. What did you find?"

"For one thing—money. Which is still there."

"And a book with notations that we can't decipher." Wyatt kept his gaze on the woman's face. "I want to show you what we found. I'm going to reach slowly into my pocket so you can see exactly what I'm doing. I'm not armed. Don't shoot me."

Moving very slowly as promised, he slid his hand into the pocket of his sports coat and pulled out the little book he'd taken from the safe. Carrie hadn't even known that he'd brought it along.

"Can you tell us what it is?" he asked.

Chapter Nine

Rita reached out and took the book from Wyatt, looking as if she was testing its weight in her hand.

"Have you ever seen this before?" Wyatt asked.

"I don't think so." She riffled through the pages, looking at the sets of numbers.

She shook her head. "This appears to be something Aaron hid from me."

"Why?"

"Maybe he was ashamed of what it represented."

"Because?" Wyatt pressed.

Carrie's breathing stilled as she waited to hear more.

"I think these are notations of his gambling wins and losses," Rita said.

"Gambling?" Wyatt asked, clearly surprised by the unexpected answer.

As Rita put the gun back into the drawer, her expression turned sad. "I didn't know it when we married, but he was heavily addicted. At first he won, and I wondered where he got the extra cash, since he couldn't be making that much money as a junior prosecutor. We had a confrontation, and he bragged about how good he was at picking horses and playing blackjack. Then his luck changed. He never talked about it, but I knew from the way he was acting.

"I suspected he owed a lot of money. I was so frightened about what would happen if he couldn't pay. I begged him to get help, but he wouldn't do it. That's why I left him."

Carrie thought about the woman's family background. "Couldn't your parents cover his debts?"

"I'd asked them to bail him out a few years ago. They'd made it clear that they wouldn't do it again."

Carrie nodded.

"So he might have done something for money—something that he wouldn't have considered under other circumstances?" Wyatt pressed.

She gave him a pleading look. "I don't know. I didn't want to know." She clenched and unclenched her fists. "Once he sold a piece of jewelry that had been in my family for generations. After that, I put my valuable pieces in a safe-deposit box—one where he didn't have the key."

Carrie nodded sympathetically.

"It was like he was on drugs," Rita went on, speaking more to herself than to them. "A sickness he couldn't free himself from. I tried to help, but I couldn't reach him. Not on that."

Carrie put a hand on her arm. "We're both sorry to be pressing you, and I'm sorry that we made up a story about Wyatt's knowing your husband, but we're in a terrible situation. In the last few days, there have been two attempts on our lives. We're trying to figure out who's behind the attacks. I mean, besides the obvious answer of the terrorists."

"I can't imagine what you're going through, and I'm sorry I pulled a gun on you."

"It's understandable," Wyatt answered, "given that the cops are making it look like we're suspects. Did they tell you anything they haven't said in public?"

"No. Just that they wanted to talk to you about… what happened last night."

Wyatt's expression turned grim. "I think we'd better leave," he said. He gave the widow a direct look. "They may be looking at security tapes from the building, and they may ask what we said to each other. I'd appreciate your not telling them we were here. But if you're forced to, you can say we came here looking for information." He fixed his gaze on her. "Did you talk to the police about Aaron's gambling problem?"

She flushed. "No."

"You might want to tell them."

"Why?"

"It gives them another motive for his murder— one that doesn't lead back to us."

She nodded. "You said there was money in the safe? Could you give me the combination?"

"Yes." Wyatt gave her the numbers and the directions, which she wrote down on a piece of paper and put in the drawer with the gun.

"Thank you."

Carrie stepped forward and hugged her. "I'm so sorry for your loss, and I'm sorry that we had to approach you this way."

"I understand."

"We'd better go," Wyatt said. "And again, we're sorry for the intrusion."

"Let me go back to the living room and make sure the coast is clear," Rita said.

When she'd left the room, Carrie looked at Wyatt. "You think Aaron Madison could have told the terrorists where and when I was meeting—for money?"

"It could be. He'd do anything he had to—if the mob was going to come after him for money."

"The mob?"

"He wasn't placing bets with the Easter Bunny."

Before Carrie could reply, Rita hurried back into the room. "There's a police detective Langley in the living room."

"What's he doing here?"

"He wants information about Aaron. I hate to tell him about the gambling."

Carrie clamped her hand on Wyatt's arm. "What about us? If they find us here, they'll take us down to the station house."

"I'm thinking." He turned to Rita. "Is there another way out of the apartment?"

"There's a service door in the kitchen, but you have to get back to the living room before you can use it."

Wyatt looked at Carrie. "You can change clothes with the maid."

Carrie stared at him. "What?"

"That will get you out of here."

"What about you?" Carrie asked.

"I'm going to have to use another method." He turned to Rita. "Ask the maid to step in here." When she'd gone, he turned to Carrie. "We've got to make it look like Rita and the maid weren't cooperating with us, which will be better for both of them when the cops start asking questions."

"How?"

"We're going to force them."

Mrs. Madison was back with the maid in a few moments. When she stepped into the room, Wyatt pulled out the gun he'd concealed under his jacket.

Rita and the maid, whose name tag said Pamela, gasped.

"My partner needs to wear your uniform. Take it off," he said to the maid in a harsh voice. "You can wear my partner's clothing."

When she stared at him in dumb shock, he growled, "Hurry. We don't have a lot of time. Or do you want me to take it off of you?"

Pamela began hastily unbuttoning her uniform, while Carrie took off her slacks and jacket. The uniform was a little large on Carrie, but it would have to do.

When the clothing exchange was finished, Wyatt turned to the maid. "Get in the bathroom and stay there. You, too," he said to Rita. "And keep your mouths shut for the next twenty minutes."

She looked shocked but did as he'd asked.

When he'd closed the door behind the women, he turned to Carrie.

"Walk down the hall to the kitchen, and leave the apartment through that door. Exit the building through the service entrance," he said to her. "Meet me at the car."

She answered with a tight nod.

Wyatt grabbed a chair and tipped it up so that the back held the bathroom door closed. Then he turned back to Carrie.

"You'd better get going."

Her heart was pounding as she asked, "How long should I wait at the car?"

"No more than ten minutes. If you hear sirens, get the hell out of here."

"I—"

"Go."

She gave him a fierce hug, then made herself step away. Everything they did was crumbling into a mess, but she wasn't going to just turn herself in to that detective in the living room.

Trying to look normal, she walked down the hall. When the police detective's gaze flicked her way, she forced herself to keep walking, then breathed out a sigh as she stepped into the kitchen. Every moment she expected him to come charging after her, but nobody followed. With a sigh of relief, she stepped into the corridor and closed the door behind her. She should have asked where the service entrance was, but she'd been too shocked to think of that detail.

When the elevator arrived, Carrie stepped inside and studied the buttons. There was one for the lower lobby, and she thought that might be the right place. Or maybe she could go out through the garage.

At the lower level, she exited and looked around, remembering that Wyatt had cautioned her to keep her head down. She could see she was definitely in a service area. Upstairs, there had been marble, polished chrome and the smell of air freshener. Down here, there were cinder-block walls, cement floors and the smell of laundry detergent. A sign had various directions on it—pointing to the laundry room, the trash room, the storage room, the garage, and deliveries.

She could get out through the garage or the trash room. Which was better? she wondered as she headed down the hall. Probably she'd encounter fewer people in the trash room.

The sound of voices stopped her, and she stepped around a corner as two women in maid's uniforms passed. They paid her no attention, and she walked right on past.

Praying the cops hadn't stationed someone to guard the exit, she stepped inside the trash room. Nothing assaulted her but the smell of ripe garbage.

At the other end of the room was a door that led outside. As she entered a rectangular area at the end of a wide driveway, she let out the breath she'd been holding. She'd feared she wouldn't get out of the building, but here she was in the open air. Still, she couldn't let down her guard. Surely there was a camera out here. Forcing herself not to run, she walked up a ramp and found herself in an alley between two apartment buildings.

After hurrying down the narrow cement lane to the street, she paused to get her bearings, then decided that the car must be on the street to the right.

She'd been terrified that she'd be caught before she could get away. Now that she was outside, she found herself praying that Wyatt would show up quickly. If she reached the ten-minute limit, she'd have to decide what to do.

That was the least of her problems, she realized, as she spotted two uniformed officers walking down the street checking the license plates on the cars.

UPSTAIRS, WYATT WALKED to the sliding glass doors that made up most of the bedroom wall.

When he opened the curtains, he found a wide balcony with a couple of expensive patio chairs and a table between them.

He opened the doors and stepped out, looking down at the three-story drop.

Wishing he'd come prepared, he scanned the bedroom and saw nothing immediately useful. With a grimace, he glanced at the bathroom door, then he stripped the spread off the queen-size bed and pulled the top sheet free.

But now what? He had one sheet and three balconies before ground level.

Using his teeth, he started a tear in the fabric, then ripped it in half. He took the two halves outside and tied one to the railing, testing the knot. If he fell, it was going to be a long drop to the ground.

But he had no other options at the moment. The women in the bathroom could start yelling. Or the cop in the living room could come back to find out what was keeping Rita.

When the knot on the sheet held, Wyatt pulled it into a narrow rope. With the second sheet tied around his waist, he stepped off the side of the balcony, using his legs to take some of the pressure off his arms. Still, the bullet wound stung as he descended to the next level down. Glancing at the curtains on the bedroom window, he saw that they were closed and thanked God for small favors.

There was no way to get the first half of the sheet free, so he had to leave it where it was like a signpost announcing his escape route. With a grimace, he tied the second sheet to the current railing and repeated the procedure, climbing over the side and lowering himself down as fast as he could.

A muffled scream made him almost let go of the sheet as he reached the balcony below. Looking toward the window, he saw an elderly woman dressed in a bra and panties standing inside the bedroom staring at him in horror.

"Sorry," he called out and turned quickly away. He didn't have another rope, but he was close to the ground. Probably the woman was calling 911, he thought as he climbed over the railing and lowered himself as far as he could before letting go. He landed on the lawn at the side of the building and wavered on his feet.

Thankful that he hadn't twisted an ankle, he took a moment to straighten his clothes, then headed for the street where he'd left the car, praying he was going to find Carrie waiting.

Chapter Ten

Carrie was nowhere in sight.

Wyatt's heart started to pound again as he saw instead two cops standing near the car. The car that had an assault rifle hidden in the trunk.

Taking a deep breath, he reminded himself that the officers didn't have X-ray vision.

Were they responding to the woman who had seen him come down the building? Had the detective upstairs come into the bedroom, found the women in the bathroom and called for backup? Or did these guys just happen to be checking the area? If he turned around and headed the other way, he'd seem suspicious. If he kept walking toward them, they might recognize him, but he figured his best option was to keep going.

Trying not to look as though his heart was racing, he passed the car. Once he'd gotten by the cops, he started trying to figure out where Carrie might be. Probably she'd seen the uniforms, too, and walked past. That was, if she hadn't already been arrested.

He couldn't stop doubts from chasing themselves

around in his mind. He was supposed to be protecting her, and he'd gotten them both in a mess of trouble by going to Rita's apartment. The way he had two years ago in Greece by sleeping late when he should have been on his toes. That slipup had cost his partner her life.

He shuddered. This wasn't like that at all. He hadn't made a mistake because he was too involved with Carrie. He'd wanted information from Rita Madison, he'd taken a calculated risk and he'd learned something they didn't know before.

And now he had to find Carrie.

Trying to think the way she would, he headed for the shopping center, cursing himself for not giving her one of the untraceable cell phones. But when they'd left on this fact-gathering expedition this morning, he'd assumed they were going to stay together.

He reached the shopping area and started looking in stores.

As he walked past a coffee shop, Carrie came out, still wearing the maid's uniform, as he'd assumed she would be.

He felt a flood of relief as he saw her and noted his own profound relief mirrored on her face. Their eyes met, and he fought the need to stop and take her in his arms. Instead, he kept on walking, hoping the moment hadn't called attention to them.

She fell into step behind him as he kept moving down the street toward the main shopping area, hoping he looked as if he was a guy out killing some time—or maybe picking up something for his wife. When he turned into one of the upscale department stores, she followed him.

He paused inside the doorway, looking around as though he was trying to locate a particular department.

Several shoppers passed, and Wyatt pretended that he and Carrie had simply come in at the same time.

When they were alone for a few moments, she spoke. "What are we going to do?"

"Better not to be seen together. You spend about five minutes in the ladies' room. I'm going back to the car and hope that the cops have moved on. I'll drive over and pick you up at this exit."

She looked down at her clothing. "I'm wearing a maid's uniform."

"Maybe you're out shopping on your lunch hour. You can change into something else later."

A woman with a shopping bag was approaching the exit where they stood, and he stopped talking abruptly.

As though they'd simply bumped into each other casually, Carrie nodded at him and started walking toward one of the clerks at the jewelry counter, where he presumed she was asking for directions to the ladies' room. He walked toward the shoe department, stopped to look at a couple of oxfords, then exited the store. Turning back the way he'd come, he headed for the car. As he approached, he saw that no one was paying any attention to the vehicle. Was it a trap?

If he'd had an alternate means of transportation, he would have left the car where it was. But he hadn't even thought he'd need one false identity—let alone more. The alternate driver's license and credit card had simply been a precaution. Renting another vehicle under the same name wasn't going to help. And stealing a car was too risky.

After unlocking the car, he climbed in and sat for a moment gripping the wheel before pulling out of the parking space and heading back the way he'd come. When he slowed near the store exit, Carrie came out and looked right and left before walking rapidly toward the vehicle and climbing in. Before she'd had a chance to buckle her seat belt, he drove off, turning down Western Avenue and then into a residential area.

Carrie sat with her head back and her eyes closed, and he couldn't stop himself from reaching over and laying his palm over her clenched hands. She knitted her fingers with his, holding on tight.

"I was scared," she finally said.

"So was I. When I came back to the car and found you weren't there."

"And I was frightened for you. What happened upstairs? How did you get away?"

"I tore up a sheet and used it to climb down from the balcony."

She sucked in a sharp breath.

"I made it." He laughed. "After I scared the bejesus out of an old lady in her underwear two levels down."

Despite the gravity of their situation, Carrie laughed, too, and he liked the sound.

Wyatt kept driving, making several turns past upscale houses with well-kept landscaping. As far as he could see, no one was following them, but there was one more thing he had to check. He found a driveway with tall hedges on either side and pulled in.

"What are you doing?"

"Making sure nobody put a tracker on the car."

"Could they do that?"

"It's not likely, but I need to be certain," he said, thinking that a lot of things that weren't likely had happened since he'd taken the job of protecting Carrie Mitchell.

CARRIE WATCHED WYATT get out of the car. Bending over, he ran his hand under the front bumper and along the sides, moving slowly and repeating the process in back and on the other side.

When he got back in, he looked relieved. "I think we're okay."

"Are we?" she asked, not just thinking about the transmitter.

They were sitting in a car screened by tall bushes on each side, making a private little enclave on a residential street. Before he could start the engine again, she shifted out of her seat and reached for him across the console.

Would he resist the embrace? She held her breath, waiting to find out what he would do. To her relief, he leaned into her, sighing as he gathered her closer.

"Lord, Carrie," he murmured as he ran his hands up and down her back and into her hair.

"I was so worried about you," she whispered.

"Yeah. Likewise."

She was so relived he was all right. That she was all right. That they were back together again. And all she could think about was getting close to him, feeling the reassurance of his arms around her again. Craving as much of him as she could have, she hoisted herself over the console, into his lap. Because his legs were long, his seat was far enough from the wheel to make room for her.

She had never been wild and reckless, but she felt that way now. Without giving herself time to change her mind, she straddled his lap so that the hot, needy place between her legs was pressed to the front of his jeans.

He made a strangled sound. Before he could change their positions, she tipped her face up and found his mouth. The moment their lips met, the kiss turned so hot that it could have started a wildfire. The morning's adventure had driven both of them to the edge of desperation.

What she needed was to close her eyes and focus

on the man who held her in his arms instead of everything else that was happening to her.

He sipped from her mouth, then deepened the kiss. She loved the taste of him, the feel of his body, the way he clasped her tightly. She'd been craving this since last night, and the terror of the past few hours had only intensified her emotions.

She forgot where they were, forgot everything except the need to get close to him—as close as two people could get.

His tongue dipped into her mouth, exploring the line of her teeth, then stroking the sensitive tissue on the inside of her lips, sending hot currents curling through her body.

She knew he had tried to keep his distance from her because he thought it was the right thing to do. And she knew now that he had given in to the heat building between them. His hands stroked up and down her ribs, gliding upward to find the sides of her breasts, then inward, across her nipples. At the same time, she felt the erection that had risen behind the fly of his jeans pressing against the part of her that needed him most.

Earlier she'd been wearing slacks, but the maid's uniform was more convenient. If she took off her panties and unzipped his fly, they could do what they both craved.

Her breath shuddered in and out as he undid the buttons at the front of the dress and slipped two fingers inside, dipping under her bra to stroke her nipple, sending heat shooting downward through her body.

She could do the same thing, she thought, as she unbuttoned the front of his dress shirt enough to ease her hand inside, playing with his crinkled chest hair. She found a flat nipple, feeling it stiffen at her touch. Sliding back a little, she reached for his belt buckle.

Before she could undo it, the sound of a car horn went through her like a shock wave.

Chapter Eleven

Jerking away from Wyatt and back into the passenger seat, Carrie looked wildly around for the source of the intrusion into the private world they'd wrapped around themselves and saw a Cadillac in the street behind them. As she turned to stare, the woman driver honked again.

Wyatt swore under his breath, turned the key in the ignition and backed out of the driveway, easing around the luxury car.

An older woman with dyed blond hair was staring daggers at them. Rolling down her window, she stuck her head out and called, "How dare you use my driveway for a dalliance with the maid!"

"The maid?"

Oh, right. She was still wearing the borrowed uniform.

Carrie felt her cheeks flame and ducked her head, trying to hide her face.

Wyatt slammed the gearshift into Drive and pulled around the circular driveway, his mouth set in a grim line.

"I'm sorry," she whispered.

"Not your fault," he answered as he sped away. "That wasn't going much further anyway. The first time I make love with you, it's not going to be in the front seat of a car in someone's driveway."

She digested that comment. "Did I hear you right?"

He gave her a sheepish look. "I didn't mean to say that."

"But it's what you were thinking."

"Forget it."

"I don't think so."

She wasn't going to forget something like that, because it was too good a window into his state of mind.

Wyatt wanted to make love to her. And he would. It was just a question of when.

She could continue the very interesting conversation, but she didn't think that would get her anywhere. Instead, she filed it away for future reference. Very near future.

Changing the subject, she asked, "What did I miss upstairs after I left?"

"Just my daring escape."

She felt a shiver go through her. He might joke about it, but it had been a very risky way to get out of the apartment.

"I made it," he said, as if reading her thoughts.

"Thank God. But now what are we going to do?" she asked.

"Try another approach." He turned his head toward her for a moment. "Would you have called Patrick Harrison if I hadn't gotten back to the car?"

"I don't know."

"But you were thinking about it."

"What should I have done if you hadn't come back?"

She saw him tighten his hands on the wheel, then deliberately relax them. "Withdraw a bunch of money from your bank account. Disappear."

"I don't know how to do that."

"You're smart. You'd learn," he said, but she wondered if he really believed it.

"You can't disappear forever."

"Some people do. Like that woman who was in the Weather Underground who made a new life for herself. Or that mob boss who vanished for a decade."

"Then you read years later that they were captured."

"Or not. There are plenty you *don't* read about."

"Maybe you'd better give me some tips. You know, in case I actually need to do it."

"Go to a rural graveyard, find a child born the same year you were and died when she was a few years old. Take her identity. Then move to another location where nobody would know about her. After that, say you lost your Social Security card and need a new one."

She shuddered. "That's awful."

"It works." He cleared his throat. "Back to Patrick. I don't trust him."

"Why not?"

"Because I don't trust anybody. And because he's close to this situation."

"That doesn't make him guilty. And I know he wouldn't do anything to harm me."

"Are you sure?"

She gave him a sharp look. "As sure as I can be of anyone. I told you—we grew up together."

"And you always got along?"

"Didn't we already talk about this?"

"I'm trying to get as much information as I can. I want to go back and question your father's maid—and see what I can get off his computer. And I'm not sure I want Patrick around when we do it." He checked the rearview mirror. "Give me some more background on him."

She thought back over the years that they'd been together. "There was a period when he was a teen-ager when he…resented my father, and he did some things that you could consider rebellious. But I did, too."

"Like what?"

"Him or me?"

"Both of you."

"There was a boy in school that I liked. I sneaked off to see him and had a girlfriend cover for me."

"That's it?"

"Do I have to tell you everything?"

"No." He glanced over at her. "What about Patrick?"

"Maybe the worst thing he did was borrow one of my dad's cars—and drive it up on a curb. He whacked up the axle, and then he asked me to help him get it fixed without my dad finding out."

"Did you?"

"Yes."

"Nice of you."

"He'd done things for me."

"Like what?"

She sighed. "Once when I was in sixth grade, I didn't want to go to school. I got him to help me put a thermometer on a lightbulb, then cool it down again so it looked like I had a temperature of a hundred and one."

He laughed. "You needed Patrick to help you do that?"

"Well, he caught me in the act, and then he said he wouldn't tell my dad." She swung her head toward him. "Your turn. What did you do bad?"

"So you can hold it over my head?"

"I don't want to be the only one confessing."

He thought for a moment. "There was a kid in my neighborhood who organized a bunch of us to steal car radar detectors and GPSes."

"Did you get caught?"

"I felt bad about it and quit."

She knew they were both using the conversation to keep their minds off their current problems.

"And what else? Did you seduce lots of girls when you were a teenager?"

"Actually, an older girl seduced me. Since you opened up the subject, who was your first? Not Patrick, I hope."

"I told you, I didn't think of Patrick that way. It was a guy in college," she said in a clipped tone.

"A one-night stand?"

"No. We had a relationship. Then he decided it wasn't working out."

She hoped from the way she'd said it that he'd take the hint and stop the interrogation. "How did we get into this?" she muttered.

"We were trying to decide if we could trust Patrick. You think that if we went back to your house, he wouldn't tell the terrorists you were there?"

"He wouldn't."

"*You* may be certain of that. *I'm* not taking a chance with your life. I want to talk to the maid, and I don't trust him to know where you're going to be."

"Then what are you going to do?"

"Get him out of the house. I want you to call him and set up a meeting."

"Where?"

He looked around. "We're near the Macomb Street playground. That's probably as good a place as any.

We can scope it out first to make sure it sounds like a legitimate location for a meeting."

They drove down Connecticut Avenue, then turned onto Macomb Street. The tree-shaded playground was empty, and Wyatt found a nearby parking spot.

"Be right back," he said, getting out to look around the area.

When he returned, he said, "Tell him that you're alone and that you'll meet him in an hour at the closest picnic table to the gate." He gave her a direct look. "Can you say that without making him think that you have no intention of showing up?"

"Yes," she snapped.

"And see if you can make sure Inez is there."

"I know what I'm doing."

When he handed her the cell phone, she dialed her home number.

Patrick answered immediately.

"Carrie?"

"Yes."

"Where are you?" He sounded on edge.

"I'm in D.C."

"At your apartment in Columbia Heights?"

"No."

"You should come home."

"You know I can't. It's not safe for me to go there. The terrorists could be watching the place, but you can meet me."

"Where?"

"I'm at the Macomb Street playground."

"A playground?"

"It seemed like a place nobody would look for me."

"Is Hawk with you?"

She glanced at Wyatt. "I'm alone."

"Why?"

She kept her voice even. "We decided that it would be better to separate for a while."

"I thought he was sticking to you like glue."

"I'll tell you about it when we meet."

"When?"

"I can't stay around the park—or anywhere else—too long. I'll leave and come back in about an hour. Can you get here then?"

"Where is it?"

She gave him the directions, then stumbled a bit before she asked, "Uh…who will be in charge at home, in case the kidnappers call?" As she said the last part, she felt her chest tighten. She'd been keeping her mind off of what might be happening to her father, but she'd just brought it front and center.

"Inez will be here," Patrick answered.

Carrie glanced at Wyatt and knew he'd heard.

"There's been no word about Dad?" she asked, fighting to keep her voice even.

"No. I'm sorry. Carrie…"

Wyatt squeezed her arm. When she turned to him with a questioning gaze, he pointed to his watch.

"Get here in an hour," she said to Patrick.

She hung up before he could say anything else, then glanced at Wyatt. "Was that okay?"

"Yeah, but I didn't want him to get a fix on this phone."

She nodded.

He started the engine. "The sooner we get to your house, the better. When he realizes you're not at the park, he'll come tearing home. We don't want to be there when he does."

PATRICK HARRISON PUT down the receiver, fighting to control the trembling of his body.

Carrie had vanished from the face of the earth, and he'd been terrified that she wouldn't get in touch with him. He'd told himself he knew her very well. He'd come to realize that she wasn't as reliable as he'd like.

But she had finally called, and his spirits lifted. Things were definitely looking up.

He paced back and forth, debating what to do. It looked as though his best bet was to simply meet— and take it from there. He'd have liked to get her away from the park before Wyatt Hawk came back, but he realized that the chances of keeping her out of the clutches of her bodyguard were slim.

He turned around to find the housekeeper, Inez, watching him.

"Is there any news?" she asked.

"No. I'm going out."

"Where?"

"It's better if I don't tell you," he said carefully.

"All right," she answered in the same tone, her gaze fixed on him.

He'd never been entirely comfortable with the woman, because he'd never been sure of her loyalties or her motives. Now he wanted to tell her to clear out, but somebody had to be at the house. He could feel her gaze on him as he exited the room and headed for the garage, where he'd parked the Lexus sedan Douglas Mitchell had bought him. It wasn't the car he would have chosen for himself. But that was the way the old man operated. He thought he knew best, and he didn't care what anyone else thought. Which might have been the reason he'd gotten himself kidnapped.

CARRIE TRIED TO calm the beating of her heart as Wyatt headed up Connecticut Avenue toward Chevy Chase Circle.

When he pulled into a gas station she looked at him questioningly.

"What are we doing?"

"Do you want to go out there in a maid's uniform?"

She'd forgotten what she was wearing and glanced down at herself. "Right."

"You can change in the ladies' room."

He popped the trunk, and she opened her suitcase, taking out jeans and a T-shirt. When she came back out, she stuffed the uniform into the suitcase and climbed into the car again.

As they headed for Potomac, Maryland, she felt her nerves jangling. She hadn't been home since she'd made a quick trip to the family estate after the terrorist incident. Wyatt hadn't wanted her to go back to her condo, so she'd gathered up some clothing from her old room and stuffed it into a suitcase, under Wyatt's watchful eyes. Back then he'd made her uncomfortable. Now she thought she understood him better. He was opening up in ways she never expected. More than opening up. That unguarded comment about making love to her had floored her. She was going to have to make sure he didn't forget about it. Actually, thinking about how to get him into bed was a lot more pleasant than thinking about the coming meeting with Inez. Carrie had always thought she and the housekeeper got along, but had she been wrong about the relationship all along? She didn't know whom to trust anymore.

"What do you know about Inez?" he asked as they drove.

"She's from Nicaragua. She came here on a work visa fifteen years ago, and my father got it extended so that she's a permanent resident."

"She's been with you fifteen years?"

"Yes."

"Is she married?"

"I never heard that she was."

"She left a husband and a son back in Nicaragua."

Carrie's head whipped toward him. "You know that how?"

"I had her checked out."

"Then why were you asking me what I knew about her?"

"To see if she'd told you the whole story. Do you think your father knows about the husband and child?"

"I…don't know. He never talked to me about it," she added, wondering if he'd kept the information to himself. Or if maybe he'd used it to keep Inez in line.

She knew he was ruthless, and using private information wouldn't bother him.

"Maybe she didn't abandon them," she said, defending Inez. "Maybe she sent money home to them."

"I found no record of that."

Carrie glared at him. "You were thorough."

"That's my job. Would she take drastic measures if she thought your father had dug into her past and was going to send her home?"

"You mean like cook up a terrorist plot? Then have him kidnapped? That sounds far-fetched. Where would she get the contacts?"

"It sounded far-fetched that a Federal prosecutor would take money to tell someone when you had a secret meeting downtown. But it looks like that's what happened. What if someone forced Inez to work with them?"

"Let's not assume the worst."

"You know I always assume the worst."

"What else do you know about Inez that's bad?" she challenged.

"Nothing," he said curtly, looking annoyed as he kept driving, but she wasn't going to apologize for asking her questions. He was the one who had started the conversation.

They rode in silence the rest of the way to her father's house.

Long ago, Potomac had been the home of big estates, horse riding and fox hunting. Gradually, most of the exclusive acreage had been subdivided into developments, but there were still some big properties left, including the Mitchell estate.

Her anticipation mounted as they turned onto Trotter Hill Road.

"Why are you driving past?" she asked, as Wyatt failed to turn in at the entrance.

"I don't want anyone to know we're going to your house, and I don't want to get trapped."

"You think someone is watching the property?"

"Again, we need to make the assumption."

He went an eighth of a mile down the road and turned in at their nearest neighbor's house, where there was a big for-sale sign at the end of the driveway.

"It belongs to the Butlers," she said.

"I know. I checked it out. The husband died, and the wife moved to Florida."

"What, did you check the whole neighborhood?"

"Just the properties on either side of your dad's. Mrs. Butler is holding out for her asking price. But she was too cheap to hire a security company to keep an eye on the place."

They parked around the back of the house.

"And I suppose you also figured out the best route to get there from here?" Carrie asked.

"Yeah. Around the bramble patch, not through it."

They walked past the swimming pool, across the manicured lawn and onto the rougher, unkempt fields beyond, skirting the bramble patch Wyatt had mentioned.

"I used to pick raspberries and blackberries here," Carrie murmured.

"Enough for a pie?"

"Sometimes. And they were good on my cereal in the morning."

"Patrick doesn't exactly seem like nature boy. Did he go berry picking with you?"

"Sometimes."

"So he's been out here?"

She nodded, wishing that everything didn't have a sinister implication.

They walked through a stand of white pines that had been planted long ago to shield the Mitchell property from the neighbors' view, then paused at the edge while Wyatt pulled a pair of binoculars from a knapsack he'd brought along.

"Where did you get those?"

"The same place we bought the clothes. They're not the best model around, but they'll do."

He scanned the house. "It looks quiet. I haven't been inside, except that time you stopped to get your clothes on the way to the safe house. The bedrooms are in the wing on the left, correct?"

"Yes."

"And the breakfast room is in the middle."

"Overlooking the pool."

"I don't suppose the back door is going to be unlocked."

"It shouldn't be."

He scanned the property again. "The garage door is open, and it shouldn't be, either."

"I guess Patrick was in a hurry to get to the meeting."

"We'll go in that way, but I want you to keep low as we approach. And run as fast as you can to the back wall of the house."

He went first, bending over so that running looked awkward, but she followed his example, darting around the pool area to the side of the house and then the garage.

There was no sign that anyone had spotted them. Was Inez even here?

Inside the garage, Wyatt asked, "Where is the housekeeper likely to be?"

"Anywhere. She's either working or resting."

Wyatt walked quietly to the door that led to the house. It was locked, but he took a credit card from his wallet and inserted it between the door and the jamb. After a few moments, the door opened.

"Not very secure," Wyatt muttered.

"There's a dead bolt. Patrick must have left it open."

As they stepped into the mudroom, Carrie fought a strange sensation of detachment. She'd lived here most of her life, yet now she felt totally divorced from the house. When she got out of this mess, would she even want to come back here?

And why not? she asked herself, knowing that it had something to do with Wyatt. He hadn't said so, but she sensed that he didn't approve of her father's lifestyle.

They were moving quietly down the hall when a door opened and they came face-to-face with Inez, a small, plump woman with graying hair pulled back in a bun. She was wearing a black uniform not unlike the one that Carrie had put on at the Madison house. The housekeeper screamed when she saw intruders in the house and tried to slam the door, but Wyatt caught it with his hand and held it open.

"Stay here," he ordered.

"Madre de Dios," she said when she realized that Carrie was one of the intruders. "What are you doing here?"

"We need to look around here."

"But Mr. Patrick was going to meet you."

"How do you know?"

Inez's face flushed. When she spoke, her Spanish

accent thickened. "I was listening to the conversation. I was worried about you, and I wanted to talk to you, but I knew I couldn't do it."

Carrie answered with a tight nod.

"Do you often listen in on private conversations?" Wyatt asked.

"When I'm concerned about Señor Mitchell and Señorita Carrie."

He kept his gaze fixed on her. "So you know what's been going on?"

"You mean that Señorita Carrie was attacked when she went downtown. And, of course, I know about Señor Mitchell being kidnapped."

"Were you here when it happened?"

She shook her head. "No. I was out getting groceries."

"Convenient," he answered.

Inez raised her chin. "What is that supposed to mean?"

"That you might have wanted to be out of the house during the abduction."

"How would I know there was going to be an abduction?"

"You tell me."

"I didn't." Her voice quavered, and she sounded on the verge of tears.

"It's okay," Carrie murmured. "He's just being cautious."

"*Sí.*"

"Did Mr. Mitchell know that you left your husband and child to come here?" Wyatt suddenly asked.

Inez rounded on him. "I did not leave my husband and child. In my country, women have few choices. *Mi esposo* was a man who always got what he wanted. He wanted to marry another woman. He kicked me out of the house, and when I tried to get my son, he told me I'd better stay away from the house or he'd kill me."

Carrie sucked in a sharp breath. "I didn't know any of that."

"Your father knew my history. I…went through some trouble to get a U.S. work visa."

Her voice had turned low, and Carrie could only imagine what the woman had done to get out of her country.

"My sister had worked for your father before she got married, and I wrote to him. He helped me make my residency permanent. I owe him a lot. I would never do anything to harm him."

The way Inez spoke carried conviction.

She gave Wyatt a defiant look. "I have saved my money. My son is grown, and I heard from my sister—the one who is still back home—that my husband died. My son contacted her. He wants to see me, and I was getting ready to go home, but I stayed here because you were in trouble, and I wanted to help, if there was anything I could do."

"Oh, Inez, I'm so sorry," Carrie said, reaching out and folding the older woman close. They hugged tightly. "I'm sorry for what happened with your husband and your son. And I'm sorry Mr. Wyatt was... so harsh with you."

"I understand. It is his job," the housekeeper said as she stepped away and looked at him.

"Yes," Wyatt said.

"Why did you take such a chance coming here?" Inez asked again.

"I wanted to pick up my cameras," Carrie answered, the plausible reason leaping into her head.

"And we were hoping to get some information," Wyatt added.

Carrie glanced from Inez to him and back again. From the way he'd started off the interrogation, she wondered if Inez would be willing to talk to him.

He must have picked up on the look she gave him, because he said, "I'm sorry I was rough on you, but I have to be suspicious of everyone. Carrie is in extreme danger. Every time we turn around, there's a new threat."

"Sí."

"She asked Patrick to meet her in D.C. so he wouldn't be home when we got here."

"You don't trust him?" Inez asked.

Wyatt shrugged.

The housekeeper turned to Carrie. "There's something you don't know, and I don't like to tell it to you now."

"But you will," Carrie said.

Inez nodded. "It's about your father."

"Is something wrong with him?" she asked, picking up on the woman's tone of voice.

"Not something physical. He…" She stopped and spread her hands. "He's been forgetting things. He doesn't seem like his old self."

"I didn't know."

Wyatt jumped back into the conversation. "You're saying you see some…mental deterioration in him?"

The housekeeper answered with a little nod. "*Sí.* He's not as able as he used to be, and Señor Patrick has been taking over more and more of his business dealings for him."

"Handling his finances?" Wyatt asked.

"I think so." She reddened again. "You don't like it that I listen to things, but I think I have to."

Carrie tried to take all that in as she thought back over her recent dealings with her father. He'd been more brusque recently. Quicker to get angry, but she'd put that down to the physical frustrations of old age. Maybe there was more going on than she'd thought. She felt sad and worried. How would being kidnapped affect him now?

Wyatt put a hand on her arm. "We'll get him back."

"You knew what I was thinking?"

"Yes."

She looked up to find Inez watching them and knew from the look on the housekeeper's face that she noted the relationship that had developed between Carrie and her bodyguard. Apparently, Inez was right. She didn't miss much.

PATRICK HARRISON GOT up from the wooden picnic table where he'd been sitting and paced back to the street.

He'd been at the playground for twenty minutes, and he didn't like the way this was shaping up. Carrie had said she'd be here, but so far, she was nowhere in sight. Neither was her damn bodyguard.

He made his hand into a fist and punched the chain-link fence that surrounded the play area. It looked as though he'd driven all the way into town for nothing.

There couldn't be any mistake about where they were supposed to meet, could there?

He walked outside the fence and looked up and down the street. Still no Carrie. He pulled his phone out of its holster and held it in his hand. He'd tried to call back and found that Carrie had contacted him from a phone that could only make outgoing calls, so there was no use trying to find out where she was. He wanted to tell her how worried he was about her. He wanted to beg her to show up, but he simply couldn't do it—not even in this age of instant communications.

How long should he wait before giving up and going home? Or maybe she'd gotten in touch with Inez? Maybe he should call her and find out if she'd heard anything.

THE PHONE RANG and all three people in the Mitchell house went stock-still.

Hope and pain laced through Carrie as she looked at Wyatt. "It could be the kidnappers."

"I'll get it," Inez said.

Wyatt didn't have time to give her instructions before she picked up the receiver.

"Hello?"

Wyatt and Carrie both moved close to her so they could hear who was on the other end of the line.

"Have you heard from Carrie?" a voice asked. It was Patrick, and he sounded upset.

Inez clenched the receiver more tightly and glanced from Carrie to Wyatt. "No. Should I have?"

"She was supposed to meet me," Patrick said. "But she hasn't shown up, and I'm worried about her."

"I don't know anything about it."

"You sound strange."

"I'm just, you know, on edge. I'm worried about Señorita Carrie, too. And her father."

"There's no use waiting here. I'm coming home."

"Maybe she'll show up where you are. What if she comes and you're not there?"

"I'm coming home."

The line clicked off, leaving the three of them staring at each other.

"We don't have much time," Wyatt said. "He could be right around the corner."

"It sounded as if he's still down there," Carrie said.

"Unless he was calling to test Inez." Wyatt turned to the housekeeper. "You keep watch. If you see him coming up the drive, let me know. I'm going to search his room." He turned to Carrie. "You get your cameras. Well, maybe not all of them. Anything we take might have to be abandoned."

She winced. "Okay."

"While I search Patrick's room, you see if you can get into your father's computer."

"It's password protected."

"Do your best." Wyatt charged off down the hall to Patrick's room, then stopped at the door. Would the guy have some warning system or a camera in there?

He examined the closed door and the floor around it to make sure Patrick hadn't used any device to indicate an unwanted visitor.

Wyatt opened the door and stepped into the room. The shades were drawn, and he flicked the light switch so that he could look around. His first thought was that Patrick was a neat freak. Nothing was out of place. Nothing was sitting around. It could almost have been a room in a luxury hotel where people came and went without leaving their personal belongings. Scanning the bookshelves, he saw some volumes of popular fiction, separated from books on business. He ran his hands along the volumes, intent on finding out if one of them was really a hidden camera.

There were no cameras in the bookshelves, and he couldn't identify anything on the walls that was taking his picture, either. He went into the bathroom and checked the medicine cabinet, finding only the usual toiletries. Patrick didn't seem to be on any kind of medication, or nothing that he kept where a visitor could find it.

Visitor? That stopped him short. Patrick probably wasn't expecting anyone to come in here. Which might have made him careless.

Wyatt returned to the bedroom and opened the closet, riffling through the neatly hung shirts, jackets and pants, all arranged by color. He didn't know a lot of men who enjoyed shopping for clothes, but Patrick had a lot of them, and the labels were good ones. Apparently, he liked his sartorial comforts.

He should have asked Carrie what the guy did for fun. There was no indication here of what that might be.

He opened drawers, finding carefully folded underwear and T-shirts. All of them looked as though he'd gotten Inez to iron them.

In the sock drawer, Wyatt hit pay dirt. There was a slight irregularity in the shelf-lining paper, and when Wyatt lifted it up, he found a manila folder.

When he pulled it out, he found something interesting. It was a carefully compiled and annotated employment history on a security man—named Wyatt Hawk.

INEZ STOOD IN the hallway feeling sick inside. She didn't like what she was about to do, but what choice did she have?

First she peeked into Patrick's room, where she saw Señor Wyatt searching through dresser drawers. Satisfied that he was busy, she walked down the hall to the office and saw Señorita Carrie sitting at the desk trying to get into the computer.

She could have told her the password, but then she'd have to admit how much snooping she'd done around here.

She'd watched Señor Mitchell type in the letters and numbers, and when he'd been out of the office, she'd done it herself to make sure they worked.

Before Señorita Carrie could turn around and find her standing there, she went down the hall to the front of the house, where she looked out the window as she'd been instructed. She saw no cars coming up the driveway, but she didn't expect to see anyone. Not yet.

Her heart was pounding as she moved to the kitchen and checked to make sure that neither of the other people in the house was watching. When she was satisfied she was alone, she took the receiver off the hook and dialed a number.

"Hello?" a voice said.

"Is this Home Depot?" she asked.

"You have the wrong number."

"Okay. Sorry."

She hung up quickly, knowing that she had delivered the required message. It had to do with the place she'd asked for. *Home Depot* meant Carrie was in the house.

She pressed her fist against her lips, then pulled herself together and went back to the window.

Chapter Twelve

Wyatt riffled through the folder he'd found in Patrick's drawer, noting that the information wasn't totally about him. There were also several other guys who specialized in security work, but it seemed he was the star attraction.

He thumbed through the pages and found he knew some of the men. Cal Winston was a good choice for a protection detail. So was Drake Inmann. They would both have been excellent for the assignment, but from the amount of material on each, it looked as if they'd been taken out of the running early on.

He went on to his own work history, reading about his early army training at Fort Bragg. His CIA experience in a number of countries around the world. The spy operation that had gone bad in Greece was highlighted in yellow.

So they knew about his biggest failure, but Patrick had made a notation next to it, saying that Douglas had accepted Patrick's recommendation of Hawk.

Wyatt stared at the page with narrowed eyes. If this was to be believed, Patrick had been the one who'd recommended him. Because he thought Wyatt was the most qualified, or what?

A sound behind Wyatt alerted him that he was not alone. He whirled around to find Carrie standing in the doorway.

"Sorry I startled you."

"I guess I'm jumpy."

"We both are. What did you find?"

"Work experience of several security men—me included. Did you know Patrick recommended me for your bodyguard?"

"No."

"Did you have any input into the selection or talk to him about it?"

"No."

Wyatt held up the folder. "There are several other candidates in here. Good men. Why do you think he picked me?"

"I have no idea."

He wanted to ask if she thought it was because he'd made a bad mistake in Greece, but he didn't want to open the subject to discussion.

"Where did you find the file?" she asked.

"In his sock drawer."

"He was hiding it?"

"Looks like it." He switched subjects abruptly. "Were you able to get into your father's computer?"

"Yes. The password is my birthday."

"Not too original. What did you find?"

"The usual things. His list of contacts. A list of his

medications. Angry letters he's written to various companies complaining about their products and services. There's also a file of family pictures. He must have had them scanned and put into the computer."

"Anything useful?"

"The bills he paid and his bank records. It looks like some money has been moved around."

"Let me see." Wyatt put the folder back where he'd found it and glanced around the room, trying to ensure he left no trace of his search.

"Was he always such a neat freak?" he asked Carrie.

"Not at first." She stopped and thought. "My dad used to criticize him for the way he kept his room. That made him much neater."

"Kids respond to their parents in one of two ways. Either they do what's asked of them, or they do just the opposite."

She laughed. "I guess."

"Were you as neat?"

"No. One of my acts of rebellion."

They headed down the hall again. In the office Wyatt got a listing of the files and started scanning the contents. He rummaged in a drawer for a thumb drive and stuck it in the machine. He had just started copying files when Inez came running down the hall, her face a mask of panic.

"Mr. Patrick is coming up the driveway. He'll fire me if he finds out you've been here. What should I do?"

"Just act naturally, as if you've been ironing his T-shirts," Wyatt said. He hadn't copied all the files he wanted from Douglas's computer, and it looked as though he wasn't going to get to do it.

"Come on."

He shoved the thumb drive into his jacket pocket and headed for the back of the house, but it was already too late. The front door slammed open and Patrick charged into the house.

Wyatt looked at Carrie. *Where can we hide?* he mouthed.

She looked wildly around, then pointed to the back door.

"He'll see us."

"I have an idea."

Out in the front hall, they could hear Patrick interrogating Inez.

"Were they here?" he demanded.

"Who?"

"Carrie and Hawk."

"Why would they have come here?"

"You tell me."

"I...I...don't know."

"You were alone here the whole time?"

"Of course."

The voices faded as Carrie led Wyatt to a shed a few yards from the edge of the pool deck. It filled a gap in the wall of tall shrubbery that enclosed three sides of the pool. When she opened the door and stepped inside, he followed her into a small enclosure that housed the pool's pump and large plastic cans of chemicals. They closed the door behind them, shutting out most of the light.

"Doesn't he know about this place?" Wyatt whispered.

"I don't know, but you can bar the door, and he won't be able to get in."

It seemed crazy for Carrie to be hiding in her own house—from her father's chief of staff, a man she had known almost all her life. But Wyatt couldn't shake the conviction that it would be dangerous for Patrick to find them here.

Carrie rummaged through the equipment and found a metal bar, which she slipped through two slots in the door.

"This door locks from the inside?" he asked, his voice low.

"I had one of my father's workmen put it on for me years ago," she answered.

"Why?"

"You see how the pool's enclosed. When I was a kid, a friend of my dad used to visit with a big dog that scared me. I'd be in the water or on a chaise, and he'd come charging outside. If I thought I couldn't make it to the house, I'd come in here."

The sound of footsteps made Carrie stop speaking abruptly.

Wyatt listened as the steps crossed the pool deck. He reached for Carrie, thrusting her behind him and turning to face the door.

He tensed, preparing for a confrontation as the door rattled, but it didn't open.

Outside, he could hear Patrick drag in a breath and let it out. "Carrie, you're in the pool shed, aren't you? I remember you used to hide in there."

She made a muffled choking sound but didn't answer.

"Listen to me," he continued. "I made a big mistake. I helped your father pick a bodyguard, and I recommended Wyatt Hawk."

At the sound of his name, Wyatt tensed.

"I thought he was the right man, but now I think I was wrong. I'm so worried about you. Let me protect you. Or I can call one of the other guys your father was considering."

In the dark, Wyatt could feel Carrie stiffen behind him. What if she believed Patrick? What if she took him up on the offer? Was he going to have to kidnap her to keep her safe?

He waited with tension bubbling inside him.

Patrick was also waiting for an answer. To Wyatt's relief, Carrie said nothing, and Wyatt certainly wasn't going to give away their hiding place. After long, tense moments, they heard the man kick the door.

"Get the hell out of there," he bellowed.

When they didn't answer he said, "Have it your way."

He gave the door one more kick and hurried away.

"What's he going to do?" Carrie whispered.

"I think he's going to get something he can use to break in."

"He's angry."

"Yeah." Wyatt grabbed the bar from the door, turned and shoved it through the slats in back of the shed. With a mighty heave, he pulled one free and then another.

"Go out that way," he said.

She moved around him and wiggled through.

Wyatt replaced the bar in the door, then turned back to the escape hatch. He was bigger than Carrie, and he had to twist to get his body through the narrow opening, gritting his teeth as the boards scraped the arm where he'd been shot. Behind him, he heard rapid footsteps coming back, then Patrick was rattling the door, but it held.

"Come out!" he shouted.

When they didn't respond, he started bashing the door with something heavy.

Wyatt pressed the boards he'd removed back into place. They wouldn't hold if Patrick shoved on them, but for the moment they looked okay.

"Come on," Wyatt whispered. Taking Carrie's hand, he started running across the field, hearing Patrick whacking at the shed door and cursing.

They were almost across the field when the sound of a vehicle in the Mitchell driveway made him turn. He saw a green van speeding toward the house.

"Who's that?" he whispered.

She turned and followed his gaze.

"The gardeners."

"This is their regular day?"

"I don't know."

Pointing toward the woods, Wyatt motioned for Carrie to duck low and run for the shelter of the trees. He followed, staying between her and the truck.

They had just made it to the little woods when the sound of gunfire echoed behind them.

DOUGLAS MITCHELL'S EYES blinked open. He was still in the darkened room, still lying with his left hand fastened to the bed. But something was different this time.

He stayed very still, thinking about everything that had happened. Carrie had overheard terrorists plotting when she'd been taking nature photographs in the woods. She'd talked to the police, and then everything had gone to hell in a handbasket.

She'd been hiding out with Wyatt Hawk and some other men he'd hired to protect her. She'd been safe, until she'd gone down to D.C. to talk to the Federal prosecutor.

Those details had been insubstantial in his memory. He hadn't known if they were real or if he'd made them up. Now he *knew*.

His mind had been very dim, as if all his thoughts were filtering through a glass of motor oil. Now the oil had been washed away, and his mind was functioning again.

Again?

He stopped to think about that. How long had he been feeling as though everything was all balled up in his mind?

Six months. That sounded right. For the past six months he hadn't felt like himself. Then men had captured him and locked him away from the world, and he was somehow thinking straight again.

He ground his teeth together, unable to believe that his mental state was just a coincidence.

In his mind he went back over the past few months—and the past few days, and a terrible conclusion began to dawn on him.

He wanted to howl with rage, but that wouldn't do him any good. Instead, he looked around, and made a startling discovery. He knew where he was. He'd been out of this room to go to the bathroom, and the place had looked vaguely familiar. Now he knew.

This was a guest bedroom in the vacation house he owned down on the Severn River.

Good God. He was being held captive on his own property—a location that he knew well. Was there some way he could escape? Or some way he could get a message to Carrie?

There was so much he wanted to say to her. Not just about where he was being held. Things that he should have said to her years ago.

First he had to get free of this place so he could warn her what was going on. But how was he going to do it?

Chapter Thirteen

At the blast of gunfire, Carrie stopped in her tracks.

Wyatt grabbed her arm and pulled her forward, into the shadows of the trees.

Someone had arrived in a truck that looked as if it belonged to the gardeners. Whoever it was had started shooting, and Wyatt didn't know if the fire was directed at them or at Inez and Patrick. But he wasn't going to stay around to find out.

They made it into the woods, where they stood panting. Wyatt looked back toward the house and saw several men in green uniforms standing outside. The hedges around the pool prevented him from seeing Patrick or Inez.

"What if they're hurt? We have to go back," Carrie said between breaths.

"We can't."

"But—"

He shook his head, silencing her. "We have to get the hell out of here."

He led her back the way they'd come, across the

fields and into the manicured yard of the house that was for sale.

"Wait," he ordered, leaving her beside the back wall while he cautiously looked into the car.

It appeared to be untouched. As far as he could tell, whoever was shooting hadn't figured out that they'd left their vehicle here.

He came back and motioned for Carrie to follow him. They both climbed into the car, and he drove away. But he hadn't made a clean escape. As he headed away from the Mitchell estate, he looked in the rearview mirror and saw a car exit the property and come speeding in their direction. Not the green van. A different vehicle.

His curse had Carrie's head jerking toward him. "What?"

"Somebody figured out where we were," he answered as he pressed his foot to the accelerator.

Carrie swung around in her seat, her gaze zeroing in on the pursuer.

"Hang on," he advised. He took a curve at a dangerous speed and kept going. A truck was ahead of them. Wyatt blasted his horn and swung out into the oncoming lane. He made it back onto the right side of the road just in time to miss crashing into a sedan coming the other way.

Beside him, Carrie gasped, but she didn't ask him to slow down. They had come to the more populous part of Potomac, and he chose a development at random, slowing down as he turned into a street lined with large two-story houses. He followed the entrance road for several hundred yards, then chose one of the side streets at random. From there, he wound his way through the development.

"Keep looking in back of us," he told Carrie. "Let me know if you see anyone following."

She did as he'd asked.

"Nothing?"

"I don't see anyone."

He breathed out a sigh, then left the development through a back entrance and made his way toward Route 29.

Beside him, Carrie relaxed a little.

"I have to call Inez," she whispered.

"You can't."

"But—"

"It could be dangerous for her if the terrorists are there. They'd know you were in contact with her."

"They know we were there, don't they?"

"Yeah. But they don't know your relationship with her."

"You think it's the terrorists?"

"That's my best guess."

"But there was shooting. Maybe two different groups. What does that mean?"

"The cops and the terrorists? The Feds and the terrorists? Or maybe Patrick opened fire on them," he said as he kept driving. "He was pretty angry. Out of control, I'd say."

"Yes," she whispered.

"Have you ever seen him that way?" Wyatt asked.

"No."

"So maybe the pressure is making him unstable."

"Because he's worried about me and my father."

"Maybe."

She sighed. "I understand the need to let off steam. If I start screaming in frustration, you may have to gag me."

"You won't."

"How do you know?"

"You've got your act together."

"Yes, but I feel like I'm getting people killed or putting them in danger every time I turn around. I feel like I shouldn't have gone home."

She gave Wyatt a defiant look, pulled out her phone and called the Mitchell home number.

Inez answered.

"Are you all right?" Carrie asked.

"Yes. We—"

Wyatt grabbed the phone and clicked it off. "That's all you need to know," he growled.

She glared at him and he could see her struggling for calm.

"They're okay, and we got some important information."

"Like what?" she demanded.

"We have some files from your father's computer, and we know he's got—" He stopped and wondered how to phrase the end of the sentence.

"Dementia," she said.

"Not necessarily."

"That's what Inez said. She said that Patrick's been taking over more and more of his business dealings."

"We know the business part, but she might not be interpreting the rest of it correctly."

Carrie dragged in a breath and let it out. "I'm trying to remember what he's been like. I didn't notice any difference—except that he wasn't saying much. And he got angry more easily."

"That can be a symptom. But we don't really know what was going on with him. There's simply too much happening for everything to get cleared up in a few hours. We'll find out the true story when we find your father."

"And you think we will?" she asked, her voice cracking.

"Yes." He reached for her hand, lacing his fingers with hers. "I'm sorry," he whispered.

"Not your fault."

"So you don't go along with Patrick's theory that I'm the wrong man for the job?" he asked in a gritty voice.

"No! I'd be dead a dozen times over without you."

"Maybe I've been making wrong decisions that got us into trouble."

"Do you really believe that?"

"No. I think that we're up against a…conspiracy that's bigger and more organized than anyone suspected."

"A conspiracy?"

"That's the best way I can describe it."

When he pulled to the shoulder of the road and then into a clearing, she looked at him questioningly. "What are you doing?"

"Checking for a tracker again. Making sure nobody put one on our car while it was parked at that other house."

WYATT CLIMBED OUT and went through the same procedure that he'd gone through earlier. He felt along the undersides of the bumpers, then along the undersides of the chassis. He stopped abruptly when his fingers encountered a small piece of plastic that shouldn't have been there.

His pulse pounding, he pulled it out and held it up. He hadn't expected to find anything, but here it was.

Opening the door, he eased back into the car and held the thing up.

Carrie's eyes widened when she saw it. "What is it?"

"A GPS locator."

"How long has it been there?"

"You know I checked after we left Rita's apartment."

"Yes."

"It must have been put there while we were parked at your neighbor's house."

She kept staring at the thing. "Who would do that?"

"For all I know, it could have been Inez."

"When?"

"While we were busy."

"But she warned us that Patrick was coming."

He shrugged. "This is just more proof that we don't know what the hell is going on." He turned the thing in his hand. "It could have been Patrick. He could have done it before he came up your driveway."

She looked as if she didn't want to believe either alternative, but she nodded slowly.

"And he'd have good reason. You lied to him about where you were going to be, and he wanted to make sure he had his own means of finding you."

"I don't like thinking that."

"I don't like thinking any of this. I mean, as long as we're speculating…it could be the cops."

"Why would *they* do that?"

"They might want to find out what we're up to."

"Wouldn't they just arrest us?"

"Maybe not, if they thought we were involved in your father's kidnapping."

She made a strangled sound. "That's awful."

"This whole thing is awful." Something in his expression must have alerted her that another thought had struck him.

"What?"

He laughed. "I was wondering… Maybe the bad guys and the cops both showed up back there and they were shooting at each other."

She shook her head. "Yeah, maybe they can eliminate each other."

"I wouldn't count on it. Remember, a car drove away."

The conversation brought his thoughts back to Rita Madison. Like what had she said to the cop who'd been in her apartment after she told him about Wyatt Hawk locking her and the maid in the bathroom? She'd seemed to want to help him and Carrie, but he could have totally changed her mind by locking her up. He kept his gaze on the tracker, not wanting to open that line of speculation with Carrie.

One thing he knew: they had to get moving.

He got out of the car again and put the tracker on the ground. He was going to crush it under his heel, then thought better of it. Let the bastards think they'd simply stopped moving. That would give him and Carrie a head start to somewhere. After walking into the woods and setting the tracker down inside the circle of an old automobile tire, he got back into the car.

Carrie looked at him expectantly. "You want them to think it's still working?"

"Yes."

"If they had the tracker, why didn't they follow us?"

"I guess to make us think that we'd lost them. Or if there were two sets of guys at your house, one

could have the tracker and the other could have followed us."

"Oh, great." She kept her gaze on him. "Where
are we going now?"

"When we drove away from your neighbor's, I
was thinking about the Baltimore suburbs. Now I
have the feeling that's too obvious. When they realize they don't know where we are, they're going
to start beating the bushes." He flapped his hand.
"I guess we need to go somewhere I can look at the
information on the thumb drive."

"A motel?"

"Probably."

He heard her draw in a breath and let it out before speaking. "Somewhere nice. I want to feel like
I'm not a fugitive."

"What do you have in mind?"

"What about Frederick? It's not that long a drive,
and it's a tourist area with a lot of bed-and-breakfast places."

He thought about it, then punched the small city
into his GPS. He wasn't concerned with luxury ac-
commodation, but he knew Carrie could use some
kind of respite. If he'd had the option, would he have
kept the information about the tracker to himself?
Although he would have liked to spare her the worry,
at the same time he couldn't in good conscience
withhold information from her. But perhaps he could

make her hiding place pleasant. After he took care of one more problem.

When he neared Frederick, he stopped at a shopping center on the outskirts of town.

"What are we doing?" she asked when he pulled up in front of a hardware store.

"Getting some electrical tape and scissors."

"Because?"

"If they found the car, they probably also took down the license number."

She winced.

"I believe I can make it look different."

After purchasing the supplies, he drove the car to a secluded section of the parking lot, got out and examined the front license plate. The first digit was the number one, and he used the tape to turn it into an *E*. He did the same with the plate on the back. If you stood ten feet away from it, he thought, the ruse should work.

Then he headed for the old-town area of Frederick, which had been in existence since Colonial times and was at the center of Civil War activity in the state.

Like many other older communities, it had gone through a period of decline, then began to prosper again, partly due to people moving out from Baltimore and Washington, where housing was more expensive, and partly due to the Colonial charm of the downtown area, where many restored buildings housed antiques shops and restaurants.

When they drove past a Victorian house with a B-and-B sign out front and extensive gardens all around, Carrie pointed. "Try that place."

"Spur-of-the-moment decision?"

"Yes."

He slowed and pulled to a stop down the block. "We'd better get our story straight before we go in."

"Okay, what's our story?"

"We're on a road trip traveling around Maryland and Virginia. We stop when a place strikes our fancy."

"And where are we from?"

"The D.C. suburbs. I work for the government—in a hush-hush job that I don't talk about—and you... teach...what?"

"Photography. So I can answer questions if I have to." She kept her gaze on him.

"Do you remember the names we were using?"

"Carolyn and Will Hanks."

"Right."

"And we're married?" she asked.

"Do you want to be?" he countered, wondering why he had put it that way.

"Yes."

He swallowed. "Okay."

Wyatt turned around and pulled into a gravel drive, and they got out of the car together. Carrie reached for his hand as they walked toward the front porch.

A few moments after Wyatt had rung the bell, a pleasant-looking middle-aged woman came to the door.

"Can I help you?"

"We're hoping we don't need a reservation to get a room."

"Not at all. Come in."

"We're the Hankses," Wyatt said, as they stepped into a spacious front hall. He looked to the left and saw a living room furnished with comfortable couches and chairs and what looked like antique chests and tables. On the right was a dining room with several tables.

"I'm Barbara Williamson."

"Nice to meet you," Carrie answered. She then said, "We want your best room."

"Are you celebrating something?"

"Not really, but we're having a very nice road trip, and I want to continue with the top-of-the-line experience."

"Our best room is in a private building out back. Would you like me to show it to you?"

"Yes."

They followed Mrs. Williamson through a large modern kitchen to a building that might have once been a carriage house. Unlocking the door, she showed them into a two-room suite. The sitting room was comfortable and cozy. The bedroom had a wide canopy bed. And through a doorway was a large luxury bathroom with a soaking tub, a shower and a double sink.

"Perfect," Carrie said.

"We can pay in advance," Wyatt said.

"If you like. Breakfast is between eight and nine-thirty."

"Would it be possible to have a tray brought over?" Carrie asked.

"That can be arranged. What time do you want it?"

Carrie looked at Wyatt.

"Eight," he answered.

He paid in cash before they carried their luggage into the guest cottage.

"I'm sure she didn't recognize us or anything," Carrie said.

"That seems to be the case. Wait here for a minute."

She stood in the middle of the sitting room while he set one of their suitcases on a stand. Then he began walking around the little cottage. If need be, they could get out one of the back windows, he decided.

When he turned from the window, he found Carrie standing in back of him. She turned and the expression on her face told him that she was preparing to push him—and push herself.

"Is this the kind of place where you'd like to make love to me for the first time?" she asked in a breathy voice.

He swallowed hard. "I shouldn't have said that. Do you usually ask that kind of question?"

"Never. But in this case I think I have to. Please answer the question."

"Yes," he said, his throat so tight that he could barely speak. Still, his bodyguard's mind was working, and he was thinking they were at a location where it was unlikely the terrorists would be looking for them.

"You could be making a terrible mistake," he managed to say.

"I don't think so."

CARRIE HAD BEEN warned. But she stood her ground, swallowing hard as she met his gaze.

She knew he wanted her, but she wasn't quite prepared for the masculine potency of his look. Yet he made no move to close the distance between them. As she watched a muscle in his jaw clench, she knew that he would not reach for her unless she made the first move.

Was reaching for him enough? Perhaps not.

Quickly, before she could tell herself she was doing the wrong thing, she pulled off the T-shirt she was wearing and tossed it onto the floor. Then she reached around to unhook the clasp of her bra, which she sent to join the shirt.

She saw his eyes burn as they took in the sight of her breasts. If she hadn't been sure of what she wanted, the scorching look on Wyatt's face might have sent her running. Instead, in one smooth motion she slid her jeans and panties down her legs and kicked them away so that she was standing in front of him, naked.

He stayed where he was, and for a terrible moment she thought that she had made a mistake.

Chapter Fourteen

Then Carrie saw the fire in his eyes flare. He began to do what she had done, unbuttoning the dress shirt he wore and tossing it away. Next he unbuckled his belt, then slid his slacks and briefs down his legs until he was as naked as she was—and fully aroused.

"I knew you would be beautiful," he said, ending with a low sound of need as he closed the distance between them and pulled her into his arms.

It had all happened so fast that her head was spinning. The shock of his naked body against hers was like a flare of electricity between them.

She was unable to hold back a gasp as his hands caressed her back and shoulders, then slid down her spine to stroke the curve of her bottom.

She did the same, touching him in all the places she could reach.

As the two of them rocked together, they found each other's mouths in a savage kiss that had been building since the first time they had met. Only neither one of them had understood the implications of that meeting.

She kissed him with a driving need that she hoped said all the things she wanted to say to him. And he returned the passion, making the blood pound through her veins.

When his mouth lifted, his breath was ragged, and the skin of his face was stretched taut. "Tell me to stop," he said. "I can still stop if I hear you say no."

"I thought I'd already made that impossible," she answered. "What else do I need to do?"

Reaching between them, she found his erection and clasped him in her hand, feeling the hot, solid weight of him.

He made a strangled sound that ended with a laugh. "I give up. But you'd better stop if you don't want this to be over before it's barely begun."

As she dropped her arm to her side, he moved her far enough away so that he could lift and shape her breasts in his hands, then stroked the hardened tips as he slid hot kisses onto her neck and shoulders. There were no coherent words to express what she was feeling, only the low, breathy sounds of two people caught in a spiral of hunger for each other.

She forgot where they were or where they had been. Forgot everything but the taste of him, the feel of his hands and mouth on her hot flesh, the overwhelming satisfaction of being with him like this.

He took her hand and led her to the bed, where he turned back the covers. When she lay down, he followed her onto the yielding surface.

Reaching up, she stroked his face, ran her fingers over his lips, heard him draw in a shaky breath.

Slowly, almost reverently, he reached for her, holding her close and dropping tiny kisses over her cheeks, her hairline, her ears, before coming back to her mouth for a long, lingering kiss as his hands molded her breasts.

"I dreamed of all the ways I wanted to touch you and kiss you," he said in a thick voice, then lowered his head to one distended nipple.

She cupped the back of his head, caressing his thick hair as he began to draw on her. His hand sought the other peak, pulling and tugging, sending heat rocketing downward through her body.

Lost in a world of sensation, she could only lie against the pillows, her hands dallying over his back and spine.

When his mouth returned to hers, it was infinitely gentle and tender as his hands moved down her body, stroking and caressing their way to the swollen folds of her sex, sending a surge of sensation through her, making her arch her hips toward him.

He knew how to please a woman, how to feed her arousal almost beyond endurance. Her need built until she was clinging to him, calling his name, begging him to fill the empty ache inside her.

"Wyatt, I need you. Don't make me wait."

He levered his body over hers, and she guided him into her. He made a sound of gratification deep in his throat, telling her how much he needed her.

It was the same for her. She had no words to say how good this was. She could only continue to touch him and kiss him.

When he began to move, she was lost to anything but the power of this man—in her, over her, surrounding her.

He set the rhythm, and she knew this joining was too intense to last for long. The tempo quickened, lifting her to a high plane where the air was almost too thin to breathe. She clung to him, feeling her body quicken, then burst with sensations so intense that she cried out with the pleasure of it.

She felt him go rigid, heard his shout of satisfaction as he followed her into the whirlwind. They clung together as they drifted back to earth.

He rolled to his side, and she moved with him, hugging him to her as they lay together on the bed.

He gathered her close, his lips skimming her hair, her damp face, her lips.

When the cool air on her damp skin made her shiver, he reached to pull the covers over them and settled beside her.

As the silence stretched, she understood that neither of them was sure about what to say. Everything had changed. Yet at the same time, nothing had changed. For the past half hour she had thought only of him. Now reality intruded again. They were on the run from men who had vowed to kill her. And the only thing that stood between her and them was Wyatt Hawk.

He held her for long moments, and she allowed herself the luxury of drifting off to sleep in his arms. She wasn't sure how long she slept, but when the light began to fade, she woke when he started to ease away.

She reached out and grabbed his wrist.

"I'm sorry. I didn't mean to wake you."

The tone of his voice made her turn her head and look at him. "Don't say we shouldn't have made love," she murmured as he sat up.

"Are you a mind reader?"

"No, I've learned to read Wyatt Hawk."

"I was hired to keep you safe."

"You are."

"Do you call this keeping watch?"

"We're in a bed-and-breakfast where nobody knows us."

"I'm hoping that's true."

"I think we should test out the theory of whether this was a good idea or not."

"What do you mean?"

"This." She sat up and reached for him, pulling him into her arms and lifting her mouth to his.

She was shocked at how aggressive she'd become, but apparently, she was going to have to make her wishes clear, at least until they were out of danger and Wyatt stopped telling himself he was neglecting his duties.

At first, she knew he was thinking he should drag himself out of bed. But as she kissed him and touched him, she knew she was having an effect on him. And she was gratified when he let her drag him down to a horizontal position again.

She kept him busy for another hour, finding out what he liked and loving the way he returned the favor as they explored each other's bodies.

She was smiling when she finally lay back against the pillow, totally satisfied.

Wyatt stayed beside her for a few minutes, then cleared his throat. "I'd like to take you out for a good dinner, but I think it's better if I bring something back."

"Agreed."

He climbed out of bed, and she admired his body as he found his clothes and pulled them on.

"What do you want?" he asked.

"Surprise me."

He left the cottage and was gone for half an hour, during which she showered and got dressed. When he came back, she caught the tempting aroma of Italian food.

"I got veal and chicken," he said. "You can have your pick."

"Good choices. We can share."

He'd even bought a bottle of wine, which they also shared. The meal gave her a glimpse of what life could be like with Wyatt Hawk under normal circumstances.

In the next moment, she brought herself up short. She shouldn't be thinking about life with Wyatt. At least not until they'd rescued her father—and figured out what to do about the men who were after them.

But they'd made love, and she wasn't into one-night stands. She'd been thinking about the future all along. The problem was getting her dinner companion to think along the same lines.

Toward the end of the meal, he seemed preoccupied.

"Earth to Wyatt Hawk," she said.

He looked up. "Sorry. I was thinking about what I'm supposed to be doing. You know, my job."

He pushed away from the table and brought over his laptop.

As he waited for Douglas Mitchell's files to load, he said, "Keep everything in the suitcase, in case we need to make a quick getaway."

"You think we will?"

"Like I said, be prepared."

She cleaned up after the meal, then sat beside him, watching him scrolling through information, before stopping to read something more carefully.

"What?"

"I'm seeing notations of money transfers."

She leaned over and looked at the screen, which showed a spreadsheet. "From where to where?"

"I'm not sure. The institution names are coded." He looked up at her. "Would he be trying to hide money to avoid paying taxes on it?"

She sighed, thinking about his business practices

over the years. "He might. He didn't like giving the government more taxes than he absolutely had to."

"And most of his income was from investments?"

"Yes." She stared at the numbers on the screen. "I guess there's no way to figure out where the accounts are?"

"Not all the files are here. I need more information."

She stood up and paced to the window, looking out into the darkness. Had her father been doing something shady with his money? Or what if the problems Inez had mentioned were making him act erratically?

She wished they had the rest of the files, but they weren't going back to her father's house for them.

"You should get some sleep," Wyatt said.

"What about you?"

"I want to see if I can get anything more out of this stuff."

She climbed into bed, and after the day she'd had, she was asleep almost instantly.

The next thing she knew, Wyatt was putting a hand on her arm.

Her eyes blinked open, and she saw him standing beside her, wearing a T-shirt and jeans.

"Hi," she murmured.

"Sorry to wake you up, but I want to get out of here early."

"What time is it?"

"Six-thirty. Get dressed, and I'll ask Mrs. Williamson if we can eat early."

When he started to pull away, she sat up and gave him a quick kiss.

He kissed her back, but she wondered if he was regretting getting so close to her yesterday.

As he left the cottage, she climbed out of bed and stretched, then padded into the bathroom.

WYATT LEFT CARRIE in the cabin and walked through the back garden toward the main house.

He could hear classical music playing as he stepped through the back. Other guests must be up, he thought as he heard Mrs. Williamson talking to a man with a deep voice.

Then the man's words reached him, and he went very still as he heard the name Carrie Mitchell.

He couldn't hear Mrs. Williamson's response, but just the mention of Carrie's name was enough for him to know that he had to get her the hell out of here.

Either this guy was from the police or the Feds, or he was pretending to be a cop.

For several seconds he debated what to do while cursing himself for leaving his gun back at the cottage. And for what he and Carrie had been doing yesterday. He'd known it was a bad idea, but he'd let her—

He stopped that thought cold. *Don't blame that on her,* he told himself.

Quickly he backed out the way he'd come and ran through the garden to the cottage. When he burst in, Carrie was just pulling on a T-shirt.

"What?" she asked when she saw the expression on his face.

"Someone's found us."

"The terrorists?"

"I don't know."

"What are we going to do?" she asked, her voice filled with panic.

"Ambush him. He doesn't know we know he's here." He pulled the curtains aside and peered out the window, then cursed.

"What?"

"I only heard one guy talking to Mrs. Williamson, but two of them are heading this way. We're going to try to take them without shooting."

"How?"

"They think they've got surprise on their side."

He was still silently cursing as he tried to revise his plans. He wanted to send Carrie out the back window, but he had no idea if the two guys were coming in the front or if one of them was going around back. Presumably, they were both armed, and he had only one weapon. Looking wildly around, he spotted the twin brass lamps on the bedside tables. After pulling them out by the cords and popping off the shades, he kept one for himself and shoved the makeshift club into Carrie's hands.

The lamps had a longer reach than using the butt

of his gun to whack the guys. Or would it be better to shoot the bastards and run? That made sense unless it really was the authorities coming to apprehend them.

His thinking time was cut off abruptly by a knock at the door.

Ask who's there, he mouthed to Carrie.

"Who is it?" she called out.

"Breakfast from Mrs. Williamson."

Carrie glanced at him for instructions.

Stall, he mouthed.

"We're not dressed," she said. "Give us a minute."

He bent to Carrie's ear. "Open the door and step back against the wall, beside me."

Her face was pale as she approached the door. "Just a minute." Reaching out, she turned the knob and stepped beside Wyatt, who was already in position against the wall.

Two men barreled into the sitting room, guns drawn.

Wyatt took the first intruder down with a sharp blow to the back of the head, using the lamp. The man dropped with a satisfying groan of surprise.

The other stopped short, figured out the trap and tried to whirl toward Wyatt, but he tripped over his buddy, who was lying on the floor by the door. Carrie slammed him with her lamp. Wyatt gave him another blow just to make sure he was sufficiently immobilized.

He handed Carrie his gun as he stepped around the two men. "Cover them."

"Who are they?"

"We'll try to find out."

He closed the door, then bent to the unconscious men, riffling through their pockets.

Each of them had a wallet with what looked like a Federal identification card.

Carrie saw the cards and drew in a quick breath.

"They could be fake. I want to tie these guys up and ask some questions."

He was looking around for something to use when he heard the sound of police sirens in the distance.

Carrie's eyes widened. "How did they find us?"

"I didn't hear the whole conversation this guy had with Mrs. Williamson. Maybe she saw a news report about us and figured it out. Maybe she was suspicious of these guys and called the cops. Whatever's going on, we can't stay here."

He grabbed the suitcases, stuffed his laptop inside and headed for the door, ushering Carrie ahead of him. As soon as they'd gotten into the car, he started off, taking a loop road around the property. As they reached the exit, he saw a police car driving toward their cottage. It stopped, and two uniformed officers got out.

He didn't stay to find out what was going to happen next. Exiting the property, he headed toward the center of Frederick.

"How did those men find us?" Carrie asked in a thick voice.

"Like I said, if it's the cops, Mrs. Williamson could have called them. Or if it's the terrorists, when they realized the tracker was gone, they started beating the bushes."

"Like how?"

"They must have drawn a radius around where I left the tracker, then began searching places where we might have driven to."

"That would take a lot of manpower."

"Which makes it sound like they're desperate to find us."

"If we can't go to a motel or a bed-and-breakfast, what are we going to do?"

"Either find a place to sleep in the car or do some breaking and entering."

She sucked in a sharp breath. "I don't like that."

"Neither do I, but we may not have much choice."

CARRIE TURNED HER head to look at Wyatt's grim profile. "You're thinking that we could have gotten caught while we were making love," she said.

"You're damn right."

"You had no way of knowing that was going to happen."

"I told you, my job is guarding you, not setting you up to get captured or killed."

"You didn't. I was the one who started it."

"And I should never have gotten so close to you."

The words stung, but she understood where they were coming from. He'd made a mistake. Or she'd put him in a position where it was almost impossible for him to turn away from her. That hadn't been a smart move on her part. To put it mildly. But she'd wanted him, and she'd gotten what she'd wanted. At least for that moment. She hoped she hadn't won the battle and lost the war.

She cut him another glance and saw that his grim expression hadn't changed. It made her feel like she had that first week at the safe house, when he'd deliberately kept his distance from her. He was doing it again. This time she understood why.

She wanted to reach out and lay her hand over his, but she didn't do it because she knew what reception she would get. Better to try to play by his rules until this was all over. Then she could go back to where they had been. Or could she?

Beside her, Wyatt cleared his throat, and she tensed.

"I was thinking we should look for a place to hide out," he said slowly. "But now I think that won't work."

Chapter Fifteen

"What do you mean?" Carrie asked. "Where else could we go?"

"What if we went back to Rock Creek Park, to the place where you first saw those guys plotting?"

A shiver went through her when she remembered her last visit to that location. Catching her reaction, he pressed his hand over hers.

"Sorry. I guess it's not the place you'd choose to visit."

She swallowed. "Why do you want to go there?"

"Because we may find something there that we can use."

"I'm pretty sure the D.C. cops and the Park Police scoured the woods."

"But maybe they weren't looking for the right thing. Maybe if you'd been along to point them in the right direction, they would have come up with something useful."

She nodded, remembering that all she'd wanted to do when she'd heard the terrorist plot was get out of there.

"The police wouldn't let me come back."

"Because they were being supercautious."

"And we're not?"

"In this case, it's the last thing anyone would expect."

He had been heading toward Baltimore. When he came to the place where the road split, he took the Route 270 option—toward D.C.

"LETTING YOU GET up to use the bathroom is a pain in the butt," one of Douglas Mitchell's captors muttered.

"Sorry."

"Yeah, this prisoner thing is getting old," the other guy added. "Next time maybe we'll leave you to pee in your pants."

"Why are you doing this to me?" Douglas asked. "It's for money, right? I can pay you more than whoever hired you to do this."

"Shut up if you don't want to get whacked," the first one said.

Douglas clamped his lips together as he sat down on the hard iron bed while the young man fastened his arm to the side rail again. There was a metal cuff around his wrist and a metal bolt attached to the bed. But the middle part of the bond was some kind of nylon rope. The young man standing over him set down a paper plate beside Douglas on the bed. The plate had a peanut butter and jelly sandwich. Beside it was a bottle of water. The men left the food and drink, then marched out of the room. It was obvious that they'd expected this hostage situation to be over a lot sooner, and now they were taking out their annoyance on their captive.

After they closed the door, Douglas listened intently. He could hear angry voices raised, men arguing with each other.

"We were supposed to be outta here by now."

"When are we going to get our money?"

"And what about Bobby? We just leave him hanging out to dry?"

"He shouldn't have got his ass caught."

Douglas strained his ears, but he didn't hear anything else for a few moments. Then another of the men spoke up.

"I say we see how much we can get out of the old guy."

"That wasn't the deal."

"The deal is what we can make it."

There was more arguing, but they'd apparently moved too far away for him to hear clearly.

How many of them were out there? Altogether, he'd seen four, but he suspected there were more men involved.

Douglas took a couple bites of the sandwich and washed it down with some water. He hadn't eaten peanut butter and jelly since he'd been a kid. It tasted comforting, and he wondered why he hadn't asked for it more recently.

He finished the sandwich, then reached into his

pocket and pulled out something he'd found in the bathroom. A broken piece of glass that had fallen behind the toilet. If he'd been paying to have the house cleaned, he would have been angry that there was something sharp in the bathroom.

Instead, he was elated. It was a weapon, and maybe he could use it to saw through the nylon rope that held him to the bed. It would take a long time, but he had nothing but time—until these men got the word that his daughter was dead. Then they wouldn't need him anymore. He cursed under his breath, thinking of Carrie and himself. Then he firmed his lips.

He turned the rope over so that the bottom side was up. Then he laid the raw edge of the glass against the fibers and began to pull it back and forth with a sawing motion. Of course, trying to get free was risky, which was why he was working on the bottom of the rope. If his captors figured out what he'd been trying to do, they would surely punish him. Maybe even kill him. But he had to take the chance.

He glanced up, looking around the room. Could he get out the window if he freed himself? And how would he get away? He knew there was a boat down at the dock. Maybe he could escape by water. He'd have to figure out that part when he got free.

NEITHER CARRIE NOR Wyatt spoke much on the trip into D.C., except when Wyatt cursed as he hit the usual morning Beltway traffic.

She knew he was tense. She was, too, but she tried to tell herself they were doing something positive—so far as they could do anything that would help them.

They took Connecticut Avenue into the District, then turned off onto Military Road, heading for the part of the park where she'd been taking pictures when she'd heard the men talking—and disrupted her whole life.

"You were photographing an eagles' nest?" he asked, as they drew near to the picnic area.

"Yes."

"And you remember where it was?"

"Yes. I've been there a lot of times. I've got pictures of the parents getting the nest ready for laying eggs, pictures of the just-hatched babies, pictures of them growing up. I was going to do an article on the eagle family."

He nodded, and she wondered what he thought about her fascination with the eagles. Sometimes she wondered the same thing. She loved the domestic details of raptor life. But not the domestic details of human life?

Had she used her nature photography work as an excuse to stay out of relationships? She hadn't thought of that until this moment, and she mulled over the concept as she directed him to the right part of the park.

It was still early, and no one was at the picnic site. Still, as she'd expected he would, Wyatt didn't stop immediately but drove slowly past, scouting out the location.

"I parked around the other side, and came in through the woods," she said, pointing out a side road that wound through the park. It wasn't like Central Park in New York or any park that had been tamed into a human notion of what would make a good outdoor play area. Instead, most of the acreage was woodland that had been left pretty much as it had been before the city had grown up around it. There were deer, squirrels, raccoons and all sorts of wildlife in the area. Probably even coyotes that had made it that far east, although she hadn't seen any. And, of course, lots of birds.

They pulled up in a shaded area, and she led Wyatt through the woods to the huge oak tree where the eagles had made their nest about eighty feet from the ground.

"I wonder how much the babies have grown since I was here last," she whispered.

"Are they afraid of people?" he asked.

"Not really. I mean, anybody who tried to climb up and bother them would probably get their eyes pecked out. Plus the eagles are at the top of their food chain, so they're not worried about predators. There are some threats to the eggs and the young birds. Like raccoons. But the parents guard the nest. The mother's on there with them at night, and the father is on a nearby branch." She kept talking, relating more eagle facts to keep her mind off her last visit here.

But she finally asked, "The terrorists wouldn't be watching this place, would they?"

"More likely they'd avoid it," Wyatt answered.

They moved quietly through the trees, and she pointed toward the oak, then upward where the parents had built their giant nest in a triangle formed by three large branches.

Wyatt stared at the structure. "Impressive."

"It's about the size of a Volkswagen Beetle and weighs a thousand pounds."

"Hard to believe that two birds can build something like that."

"The male picks the location and does most of the nest building. And the female helps keep it in good shape. It's amazing what size branches they can bring in."

"You've obviously spent a lot of time watching them."

"Yes. And there are websites where you can read about eagle behavior. One of my favorites is in Decorah, Iowa."

"Did you name these birds?"

"I thought about it, but they're wild creatures. I called the parents Mom and Dad and the two babies RC One and RC Two."

"For Rock Creek?"

"Yes."

He nodded, looking up at the nest, but she saw he

was dividing his time between it and the surrounding woods.

As she focused on the nest, one of the young eagles moved to the very edge of the nest and looked down at them from its high perch.

Wyatt stared at the large black bird. "You're telling me that's a bald eagle?"

"Yes."

"But he's all black."

"They don't get white feathers on their heads and tails until they're four or five years old. These are only a few months old. The last time I was here, they hadn't branched yet," Carrie murmured.

"What does that mean?"

"It means fly to a nearby branch that's within easy reach of the nest."

"I guess that gives new meaning to the phrase 'branching out.'"

"Yes. That must be where it came from. After that, they fledge. Which means fly away from the home tree before coming back."

As they watched, the young bird flapped its wings and took off in a graceful glide to another tree about fifty yards away.

She and Wyatt watched it land about forty feet up on the trunk of another oak. Not on a branch that could hold its weight. Something else.

"What's he standing on?" Wyatt asked.

"No idea. There are leaves in the way."

"He wasn't over there before?"

"Like I said, the last time I was here, the juvies were too young to fly. I'd never seen any of them out of the nest until just now."

She followed Wyatt as he walked closer to the spot where the eagle perched, staring up at him. "He's not standing on anything natural," he muttered.

He moved to a different angle, and trained his binoculars on the bird.

"I can't see exactly what it is. Too many leaves."

He looked up and down, judging the distance from the ground to the first branch.

"I think I can get up there—if you give me a lift."

"Why do you want to?"

"There's just something about the location..." His voice trailed off, and he shrugged. "Can you make a stirrup out of your hands?"

"Yes."

He put down the binoculars then emptied his pockets, setting his wallet and everything else on the ground. "Ready."

She did as he'd asked, gritting her teeth as she took his weight.

"Sorry," he muttered. She struggled to hold steady while he reached for the lowest branch. He got his hands around it and began to pull himself up. When he winced, she remembered that he'd gotten shot in the arm a few days ago.

"Should you be doing that?" she asked.

"Have to."

He clenched his teeth and pulled himself up to the

branch, then climbed onto the horizontal surface. After a moment, he hoisted himself up another level.

The young eagle, who had been looking down at the man invading his space, took off, flying to another tree a little farther away.

Carrie stood back where she could get a better view of what Wyatt was doing. Her stomach knotted as she watched him pull himself to a higher level.

Finally, he was even with the spot where the eagle had been standing.

When she heard him curse, she caught her breath. "What?"

"Tell you when I get down."

He stayed where he was for several more minutes, and she wondered what he was doing.

Finally he came down, moving rapidly. When he got to the lowest branch, he used both hands to lower himself and jumped the final few feet, flexing his legs as he hit the ground. When he straightened, she saw that he had tucked something inside his shirt.

"What?"

"Come on. We're getting the hell out of here."

Wyatt put everything back in his pockets, then took Carrie's hand, leading her back toward the spot where they'd parked.

As soon as they were in the car, he drew out the thing he'd carried in his shirt.

"A video camera?" she asked.

"Yeah."

He put the camera on the console and drove away,

alternating between looking ahead and checking the rearview mirror. It wasn't until they'd turned onto Connecticut Avenue that he breathed out a little sigh.

"I guess we got away." He turned toward her. "Someone was working surveillance on the area."

"But it's not unusual to have cameras trained on eagles' nests."

"That camera wasn't focused on the nest. It was pointed toward the ground."

"But why?"

"Because whoever put it there was hoping to see something, and I don't think there are cameras stationed to catch people making out at every picnic area in Rock Creek Park."

She absorbed that information. "You mean someone else knew that the terrorists were meeting at that particular location?"

"That's one explanation."

"But if they did, why didn't they move on them? Were they waiting for evidence?"

"And you stumbled into the middle of the plot? But if they were already tracking the terrorists, that means they knew about the plot weeks or months ago," Wyatt answered.

"They'd have what the terrorists said recorded, so they wouldn't need my testimony."

"Right."

"So what's going on?"

"You could say that the terrorists didn't know about the camera. They only knew that you had stumbled into their plot, and they were desperate to stop you. Remember, one of them is in custody. If you don't testify against him, they think there's no case." He dragged in a breath and let it out. "There's another way to look at it."

"Which is?"

"That someone knew you would be there and wanted to get pictures of you."

"That doesn't make sense. Why would they do that?"

Instead of answering, he asked, "Who knew where you were going to be doing nature photography?"

"I didn't tell anyone where I was taking photographs that day. But I did talk to my father about the eagles' nest. I told him I'd been watching them, and I told him some of the same things about eagle nesting behavior that I told you."

"Interesting. Which means Inez or Patrick could have overheard the conversation."

"Yes," she whispered.

"You talked to him over the phone?"

"Yes. Also, I was out there for dinner about a month ago. Then later I came out to get some clothes I wanted. I also picked up one of my lenses."

"And you said why?"

"Maybe. I can't remember."

They were both silent as they considered the implications. Carrie watched Wyatt's grim expression as he headed toward Bethesda.

"So what if there's a conspiracy against *you?*"

She shuddered. "That would mean someone went to an awful lot of trouble."

"You have a better explanation?"

"Can we see what's on the camera?"

"Maybe." They had reached the Bethesda business district, and he slowed down, then pulled into a parking space in front of an electronics store.

"Wait here. Duck down so you're not so visible."

He got out, and she followed directions, scrunching down so that only the top of her head showed at window level. As she sat there, she could feel her heart pounding. She'd known all along that she was in trouble. It seemed that more and more stuff kept piling on.

Instead of thinking about that, she tried to focus on something constructive. They needed a place to hide out, and they had limited options. An idea struck her, but she didn't know how Wyatt would react.

When he came back, he had the camera inside a bag with something he'd purchased.

"What did you get?"

"A cable that will let me download the camera's contents to the computer—if there's anything to see."

Chapter Sixteen

"What's the chance of that?" Carrie asked.

"It depends on how much storage is in the camera. It could be like store surveillance that erases the footage every week or so."

She nodded.

"Now we have to find a place where we can look at it."

"I was thinking about that," she said.

"Where?"

"Dad owns some property on the Severn River, in Arnold, Maryland. We have a house there, where we used to spend time in the summer."

"You don't use it now?"

"I think he still likes to stay there occasionally, but I haven't been with him."

"It's a possibility, but there's a chance the terrorists could know about it. And I'd like to stay closer to the D.C. area if possible."

She nodded. "What are you thinking?"

He looked at her for a moment. "Sometimes the army clears an area of insurgents and then there's no reason to go back. We can use that technique in reverse."

"What do you mean?"

"We can go back to the Butlers' house. The one next to your dad's." He paused. "I wasn't thinking about breaking in when I did my research."

"Maybe we don't have to use the main house. There's a guest cottage on the other side of the pool."

"Do you remember if it's got a direct line of sight to your dad's property?"

"I don't think so."

"Well, it's the last place they're likely to think we'd be, so we'll take a look at it."

She sighed. "I guess breaking into the guesthouse of someone you know is better than breaking into the house of a stranger."

He stopped at a commercial area, and he pointed to the array of fast-food restaurants. "Italian last night. What's your pleasure for brunch?"

She studied the options. "Let's go with Mexican."

"I wouldn't have figured you for that kind of food."

"Why not? I spent a summer in Costa Rica. Dad sent me to learn Spanish. I know Mexican isn't exactly the same, but it's similar. Well, the rice-and-beans part."

"Why did he want you to learn Spanish?"

"It was my idea. I was in high school, but I already knew I wanted to be a photographer, and I thought I'd probably travel in Latin America."

"That's very goal oriented."

"Yeah."

They pulled into the drive-through line, ordering burritos and tacos along with large cups of iced tea.

After paying for the purchases, they headed toward her father's house, giving her the feeling that they were traveling in circles.

When Wyatt drew near the Butler property, he kept alert for surveillance, then he drove slowly up the access road. He parked in the woods out of sight of the road and turned to Carrie.

"Wait until I give you the all clear. We might have to make a quick getaway."

He left the engine running as he took a quick circuit around the house, then checked for line of sight from the guesthouse to her father's place.

Still, he didn't motion for her to get out.

She saw him inspecting the door and windows of the guesthouse, and she figured he was checking for an alarm system.

Next he stood in front of the door, and she couldn't see what he was doing.

When he stepped back, she expected him to tell her to join him. Instead, he held up his hand, and she waited while he disappeared into the house. He was back in less than a minute and motioned her to get out of the car.

She turned off the engine, pulled the keys from the ignition and joined him at the open door. They both stepped inside, and she looked around at the cozy room.

Mrs. Butler hadn't bothered to clean out the cottage. She'd left the room furnished, and Carrie saw a couch, a couple of comfortable chairs, a dining set and a kitchen area along one wall.

She set the bags of food down on the table and flopped into one of the chairs.

"Long day," Wyatt said. "And it's only noon."

She nodded.

Wyatt set the camera and his laptop on the table beside the food.

As they ate, he booted up the computer and attached a USB cable from the camera to the computer.

She moved her chair around so that she could see the screen.

"I'm going to rewind to the beginning."

For a moment, the image on the screen was only black dots, and she thought maybe there was nothing to see. Then it cleared up and she got an image of men on the ground. "The terrorists," she murmured.

"Setting things up," Wyatt agreed.

They disappeared, and there was a long stretch of nothing but birds, squirrels and deer—and sometimes Carrie taking pictures of the eagles' nest.

"They were checking up on me."

"Right."

"There was probably more than one camera, and this was the only one left," Wyatt said.

He fast-forwarded through the normal forest footage. Finally the men came back.

"Is that the day I showed up and heard them?"

"We'll find out."

Before moving out of the shot, the men glanced up at the camera and at other trees where there must have been more spy cams.

"What are they looking at?" she asked.

"Checking to make sure everything's in place."

Then she saw herself, moving through the woods, her own camera in hand as she approached the eagles' nest.

Her breath caught as she stopped short. "That must be when I heard them."

"Yeah. Which makes it a pretty good guess that they were waiting for you."

"Could they send those images to a remote location?"

"Probably."

He stood up and paced the living room. "Your overhearing them was all a setup, I think."

"But why?"

"I don't know yet."

Carrie moved restlessly in her seat. She didn't want to think about what this hidden footage meant, and she found herself searching for another subject to focus on.

She knew Wyatt wasn't going to like her next question.

Chapter Seventeen

Carrie finished a bite of burrito and looked up at the man who'd spent almost every waking minute with her since they'd gotten in that town car to go downtown.

"You told me you blame yourself for your partner's getting killed in Greece. Why was it your fault?"

It wasn't until the words were out of her mouth that she realized they probably sounded like an accusation to him.

He reared back as though she'd come at him with a baseball bat.

"That's not relevant."

"I think it is."

"Because you don't trust me?" he asked in a gritty voice.

"Because I want to hear what's making you so sure that you did the wrong thing."

He slapped his drink back onto the table and glared at her, but she didn't back down.

"What kind of assignment were you on?"

"We were posing as a tourist couple traveling around the country looking at ancient sites, but we were really tracking down a terrorist cell."

"In Greece?"

"Yeah, they thought it was a good place to hide out."

When he didn't elaborate, she prompted him. "Did you find them?"

"We traced them to a fishing village, and then we lost their trail."

"And then what?"

"We spent the night at a little pension." He kept his voice hard. "And we made love that night. Which we shouldn't have done, of course."

"Whose idea was that?"

He shook his head. "It was a mutual decision."

Getting the information was like pulling teeth because he kept stopping. And every time he did, she felt her own tension mount. But she'd started this, and she wasn't going to let him off the hook, even if she was going to hate what she heard. "And then?" she asked again.

"And then in the morning when I woke up, Gina wasn't in the room."

"You'd told her to go out and do something?"

His voice jolted up a notch. "I'd told her not to go off on her own. I'd told her to stay with me, and she didn't obey orders."

The look on his face made her insides twist, but

she stayed where she was and let him tell the rest of the story in his own way.

"We'd been talking to some of the locals, and it looked like they might have some information, if we could gain their trust. I think she had some kind of idea that she could locate the terrorists and get credit for her big discovery. Instead, she was struck by a car along the road as she was walking toward the center of town. It was set up to look like a hit-and-run accident. Two years have passed and they've never found out who plowed into her."

"It could have really been an accident."

"I don't think so. I think the terrorists knew we were getting close, and they wanted to send me a message."

"How can you blame yourself for that?"

"I blame myself for not having better control of the situation."

"It sounds to me like she had made her own decision, and you couldn't do anything about it."

"I was the senior agent. The one in charge!" he shouted.

"And you felt guilty about sleeping with her. Maybe that was unprofessional. But the rest of it wasn't your fault. She didn't have to go out in the morning. You weren't even there when she was killed."

He glared at her. "You're making assumptions."

"So are you."

When she started to speak again, he stood up and

marched out of the guest cottage. She could see him standing by the pool, his back to her and his shoulders rigid.

She knew he was angry at her, questioning assumptions that he'd carried around for the past two years, but he meant too much to her to just keep her mouth shut.

He was clenching and unclenching his fists, and she was pretty sure he wanted to drive away and leave her at the guesthouse. But he couldn't do it because he had an obligation to her and her father.

She picked up her burrito and took a bite, but the food felt like cement in her mouth. After washing it down with a sip of iced tea, she got up and went into the bathroom, where she splashed water on her face. Then she walked into the bedroom of the guest cottage, kicked off her shoes and lay down on the bed. Maybe if she wasn't in the living room Wyatt would come back inside.

When she heard him in the living room, she tensed. His footsteps stopped, and she thought he might be wondering where she'd gone. Then he charged across to the bedroom.

"Come on."

"Where?"

"I spotted Patrick's Lexus leaving the property, and I want to follow him."

She jumped up, put her shoes back on and followed Wyatt to the car.

As he took off down the drive, she buckled her

seat belt. "I thought you wanted to go back to Dad's house and get into his computer again."

"Yeah. It was a tough decision, but I decided that following Patrick is more important."

Neither of them mentioned the previous discussion, and she wasn't going back to it now.

She was glad they had something to focus on besides the two of them as Wyatt drove back toward the D.C. area, staying back so that Patrick wouldn't know he was being followed. The technique was nerve-racking, because a couple of times Wyatt lost sight of their quarry, but he reappeared again each time.

"I don't believe he's thinking about being followed," Carrie murmured.

"Why not?"

"Because he's not doing anything evasive."

"Yeah, unless he knows we're here, and he's leading us into a trap."

She sucked in a sharp breath. "Why would he do that?"

"I don't have a handle on his motivation. I only know that I don't trust him."

She nodded, trying to rearrange her picture of Patrick Harrison. She'd known him all her life, and she'd considered him a friend. But now she couldn't be sure of him. Or of Inez, for that matter.

Wyatt let a couple of cars get between him and Patrick as they merged onto the Capital Beltway, and he stayed a few cars back.

With the volume of traffic, it was easier to follow him without danger of being spotted as he headed toward the city, but Patrick got off on the exit leading to Wisconsin Avenue.

When Patrick reached the Bethesda business district, he turned off onto a side street, then slowed as he came to a Starbucks, peering in the window. He pulled into a parking garage, and Wyatt and Carrie drove past.

"I think he's meeting someone there," Wyatt said. "I'm going to find a parking place. You follow him, but don't let him see you."

"Right."

She got out and pretended to be inspecting the handbags in the window of a specialty shop.

Patrick came out of the parking garage and walked rapidly back to the Starbucks, not paying attention to anyone around him.

He went inside, and she wondered what she should do.

A few minutes later, a woman came up the block, heading for the same coffee shop. Carrie blinked, wondering if her eyes were giving her the correct image. She kept staring, unable to believe what she was seeing.

Patrick was meeting Rita Madison.

The idea blew her mind.

Once Rita was inside, Carrie edged closer, moving to the window where she could peek inside. Rita and Patrick had their heads together, speaking to each other.

When Rita started to look up, Carrie pulled back so that she was no longer visible through the window.

At that moment, she sensed someone behind her and froze.

"It's me," Wyatt whispered. As she relaxed, he asked, "Who's he meeting?"

"You won't believe it. Rita Madison. And she looks more like her old self than last time we saw her—at least the way you described her."

"What do you mean?

"She's got on makeup. And she must have had her hair done."

"Interesting. Like she's out of mourning real fast." He waited a beat and put his hand on Carrie's arm, drawing her away from the window. "If I leave you alone here for a few minutes, will you be okay?"

"Of course."

"Stay out of sight. I'll be back as quickly as I can. If they come out, go into the shop next door."

She nodded.

WYATT FELT HIS stomach knot. He was leaving her in a vulnerable position, but there were two urgent pieces of business, and he couldn't take care of both of them at the same time. Praying that nothing would happen to her while he was gone, he sprinted down the block, hoping he could accomplish his mission in time. Lucky for him that they were near the same electronics shop where he'd picked up the USB cable earlier.

He rushed through the door and stopped short when he saw several customers waiting in line.

Pushing his way to the counter, he said, "I need a GPS tracker."

"You have to wait your turn, buddy," the guy to his right said in a loud voice.

"This is an emergency," he said.

"What? Your wife is hanging out with another guy?"

"Something like that."

The clerk pointed to a section of electronics devices hanging on the wall.

Wyatt strode to them, grabbed a package and looked at the price. He also scanned the directions and found the batteries he needed. He came back to the counter and threw down two fifty-dollar bills.

"Hey, wait," the clerk called out.

"In a hurry," he shouted over his shoulder.

He was out of there two minutes after he'd entered, and he didn't know if he'd taken too much time.

His next stop was the garage where he'd seen Patrick pull in. He started jogging up the ramp, looking at the cars, opening the package as he ran. He found Patrick's Lexus on the third level and stood panting while he opened the GPS and shoved in the batteries. When a green light went on, he knelt down and stuck the thing under the front bumper, hoping that this ploy was going to work.

Again he sprinted back the way he'd come, heading for the Starbucks and wondering if he was going to bump into Patrick or Rita on the way.

He got back to find Carrie where he'd left her.

"They're still in there?"

"Yes."

She stepped back, and he took her position, watching the man and woman talking inside. It looked as though they knew each other pretty well. What the hell was going on with them?

Patrick broke off to get in the coffee-order line, and Rita sat down at a table, her back to the window, presumably so that she could keep an eye on Patrick.

There were several people in line in front of him, and he moved slowly to the front.

Behind Wyatt, Carrie asked, "Where were you?"

"Tell you later."

"Let me see what's happening in there."

He and Carrie exchanged places again. After a few minutes, Carrie backed away.

"They're pushing their chairs back. I think their meeting is over."

He took her hand and hurried her to the next shop, which turned out to sell handbags.

"Can I help you?" the clerk asked.

"I want to find something special for my wife," Wyatt said.

When Carrie gave him a questioning look, he wondered why he'd used that word. But it had just come out of his mouth unbidden.

Carrie picked up a leopard-print purse and pretended to be interested while Wyatt kept his gaze on the street.

"Isn't it pretty?" the clerk said. "It's on sale for twenty percent off."

Carrie nodded, dividing her gaze between the purse and the entrance to the coffee shop. First Patrick came out and walked back toward the parking garage.

A few minutes later, Rita emerged and hesitated. For a moment, Wyatt was afraid that the woman was going to come into the purse shop, but she kept walking down the street.

"Come on," Wyatt said to Carrie.

As he started to leave the shop, the clerk called out, "That purse is a closeout. I can give you a better deal."

"Thanks so much," Carrie answered, "but we're still thinking about what to get."

Once on the street they headed in the direction that Rita had taken, putting other shoppers between themselves and their quarry. She turned down the cross street and walked to a nearby bank, where she disappeared inside.

Wyatt motioned Carrie to a passageway between two shops, where they waited in the shadows.

"What do you think they were doing?" Carrie asked.

"I'm not sure, but I assume it's nothing on the up-and-up. I mean, how do they even know each other?"

Carrie shook her head.

Rita was inside the bank for twenty minutes. When she emerged, she wore an annoyed expression.

"I guess that didn't go well."

"Are we going to follow her?" Carrie asked.

"If we can do it without her spotting us." They trailed half a block behind as Rita walked in and out of a couple of shops, then headed for the garage where Patrick had parked.

They waited until she'd disappeared inside, then got into his rental. By the time they'd paid, Rita's car was already down the block, but Wyatt caught up and kept pace with her. The surveillance did not turn out to be particularly productive, since she was only heading back to her condo.

When she turned into the garage, Wyatt continued on past.

"Now what?" Carrie asked.

"We go back to Patrick."

"You mean follow him home?"

"I hope that's not where he's going. The reason I left you alone outside Starbucks was to buy a tracker, like the one someone put on my car. And I slapped it under Patrick's bumper."

"Good thinking."

"But I'm betting he wasn't even looking. We can follow him and find out where he's going." As he drove, Wyatt got out the other part of the device, a GPS that kept them apprised of Patrick's location. Douglas Mitchell's chief of staff was heading along the Capital Beltway again.

"He could be going home."

"We'll see." Wyatt switched the subject back to Rita. "What if Rita was feeding us a bunch of bull when we talked to her?"

"About what?"

"Everything. What if that book has nothing to do with gambling debts?"

"Then what?"

"We have to find out."

Instead of heading for the Mitchell estate, Patrick took I-95 toward Baltimore.

He skirted around Baltimore and turned in the general direction of Annapolis. Wyatt stayed well back because there was no need to keep the vehicle in sight. They could follow perfectly well using the GPS.

Carrie caught her breath as he swung onto East Oak Road.

"I think I know where he's going."

Wyatt turned his head toward her, then back to the road. "Yeah?"

"Remember I told you about the house my father

owns on the river in Arnold? This is the route you take to get there."

"Patrick's going to your father's house? That's an interesting development. Okay, tell me everything you remember about the property."

She organized her thoughts.

"It was an old bungalow that my dad bought maybe thirty years ago and fixed up. The property's worth a lot because it's right on a bluff overlooking the river. The access road is about a hundred yards long. The house is one story. There are three bedrooms and a great room. Nothing fancy. In back there's a gravel walkway and stairs that lead down to a dock. Dad keeps a motorboat there."

"Is there a garage?"

"Yes, a big detached one on one side."

"So cars could be hidden inside."

"Yes."

"Is there a lot of cover on the grounds?"

"Yes. Lots of trees and shrubs. And probably underbrush that's grown up, since I don't think Dad has a gardener down here."

They stayed well back as Patrick headed down the road, then disappeared onto a long drive winding through a wooded lot that completely hid the dwelling from view.

"What's he doing here?" Carrie murmured.

"I guess we'll find out."

Wyatt continued for another hundred yards until

he found a place where he could turn off. When he climbed out, he checked his Sig.

Carrie eyed the weapon. "You're expecting trouble?"

"I don't know what to expect. I mean, why is Patrick here at all? Did Rita send him here? Or did something he told her give him the idea?"

Carrie shrugged, trying not to think the worst of a man she'd considered a friend for all of her life.

She hadn't been to this house by the river in years, but memories came flooding back as they stepped off the road and into the underbrush. She'd loved this place when she'd been a kid. Playing in the woods. Swimming in the river. Fishing from the pier. She and Patrick had made forts in the woods. Later, when they'd gotten older, they'd been allowed to take the motorboat out on the river. In the early days, there had been no air-conditioning in the house, and they'd slept out on the screened porch.

"There's a path through the woods," she whispered.

Or there had been. When she tried to find it, she found that nobody had kept it up, and the forest had closed in around the almost imperceptible trail.

"You'd better show me the way," Wyatt said, although it was obvious he didn't like the idea of her going first.

She took the lead position and started moving as quietly as possible toward the house, avoiding brambles and patches of poison ivy.

From the road, it was an uphill slog, and Carrie tried to keep the house in sight so that she wouldn't get lost as they navigated the wilderness area.

They passed a dilapidated structure.

"What's that?" Wyatt asked.

"That was one of the forts Patrick and I built. We used to play pioneer out here."

When they reached the edge of the woods, Wyatt stopped short. The house looked deserted, and Patrick's car was the only one in sight, parked beside a large heap of brush and sticks that had been piled up in the front yard and left there. He had turned his vehicle around, making it look as if he was poised for a quick getaway.

Carrie focused on the car and breathed out a little sigh when she saw Patrick through the window. He must have stayed in there for a few minutes. Now he was stepping out.

"What has he been doing all this time?" Carrie whispered.

"Don't know. Stay here."

As he got out of the vehicle, Patrick was focused on the house, not what might be in the woods behind him.

Wyatt sprinted forward and caught up with the man while he was still twenty yards from the building.

Pressing a gun into Patrick's back, he said, "Raise your voice or make a sudden move, and you're dead."

The other man went stock-still.

"What…what are you doing here?" he sputtered.

"I'll ask the questions," Wyatt answered. "Turn around and walk back toward the woods." He emphasized the order with a jab from the gun.

Patrick's gaze fixed on Carrie, and his eyes widened.

"You."

She raised one shoulder in a little shrug.

"Move."

Patrick finally unfroze from his position. Wyatt stayed behind him, marching him into the woods, where he couldn't be seen from the house—if there was anyone inside. Wyatt still didn't even know that.

He moved around to face Patrick. "What are you doing here?"

Patrick responded with a look of panic.

"Is someone here?" Wyatt prompted.

Carrie jumped into the conversation. "Did it have something to do with Rita?" she blurted, and Wyatt gave her a quick glance, sorry that she'd mentioned the other woman's name. He'd wanted to save that information as a surprise after he'd gotten the initial version of Patrick's story.

"What about Rita?" Patrick asked cautiously.

"You met with her," Carrie answered.

The look of panic on Patrick's face changed to one of cunning.

"Don't say anything else," Wyatt advised Carrie. "I want to find out what he's got to say."

Her face contorted, and he knew she realized that speaking impulsively might not be such a good idea.

"She asked to meet with me," Patrick said.

"About what? How do the two of you even know each other?"

"After her husband died, she contacted me because she knew about your being on the run."

Patrick turned to Carrie. "She gave me some information about your father. It's right here."

"About Dad?"

Patrick put his hands up. "I'm reaching into my pocket. I won't make any sudden moves." As he put his hand in his jacket pocket, Wyatt saw Carrie step closer to the man, no doubt eager to see what he had to show her.

"Stay back!" he shouted.

But it was already too late. Carrie darted forward, getting between Patrick and Wyatt's gun.

In the next second, Patrick grabbed Carrie, holding her in front of himself as he pulled out a gun and pressed it to her neck.

Chapter Eighteen

Wyatt froze.

"Drop your gun or I'll shoot her," Patrick ordered. "And don't think I won't do it."

"Patrick?" Carrie whispered.

"Shut up," he growled, and she clamped her lips shut.

Wyatt's only option was to obey.

Still holding Carrie, Patrick bent down and scooped up the weapon. But the man wasn't very good at hiding his intentions. As he held one gun on Carrie, he raised the hand with Wyatt's gun and fired.

Wyatt was already ducking behind a tree. More bullets followed him into the woods, but he could tell that Patrick wasn't much of a shot with his left hand. Ducking down, Wyatt waited in the shadows of the trees.

Behind Patrick, the door to the house opened. Peeking from behind a tree, Wyatt saw two young men emerge, both carrying guns. They looked like the terrorists he'd seen at the Federal Building and at the safe house.

"What's going on?" one of them shouted to Patrick.

"Carrie Mitchell and Wyatt Hawk showed up. I've got her. Hawk's in the woods. I've got his gun. You can blow him away."

The idea of leaving Carrie in Patrick's clutches made Wyatt's stomach knot, but he wasn't going to do her any good if he was dead.

As he turned and ran back the way he'd come, a bullet whizzed past him, and he heard the pounding feet of the pursuers.

He ducked low, making for a tangle of brambles and diving in, scratching himself as he hunkered down.

The two men were coming through the woods, mowing down underbrush as they searched for him.

Wyatt cursed under his breath. He hadn't been sure of Patrick's role in this plot. He still wasn't sure, but he knew that the man was willing to kill Carrie to get what he wanted.

Which was?

Wyatt felt his throat constrict. In the past few minutes, it had become clear that this whole plot had been about killing Carrie, and every second that passed put her in more danger.

Desperately, he tried to figure his best course of action.

The sounds in the woods told Wyatt that the men

pursuing him had separated. From Wyatt's hiding place, he saw one of them approaching his location, but his attention was focused on something farther on—the fort that Carrie had pointed out on their way up from the road.

PATRICK MARCHED CARRIE into the house. As soon as they were inside, he said, "Take off that purse and toss it over here."

She removed the strap from across her chest, and he upended the purse onto the floor, then pushed her into a chair in the great room. "Stay there if you don't want to get hurt—yet."

She watched him sort through the contents of the pocketbook. When he found the cell phone, he slammed it against the floor, spewing out its guts.

"Is that what you used to call me and get me to drive into D.C. so you could search the house?"

"No."

"Liar. You were hiding in the pool shed, weren't you?"

She didn't answer.

There were three other men in the house watching her and Patrick. One was blond. His leg was bandaged, and he was leaning on a crutch. The two others had dark hair. Ordinary-looking young men, all of them. She recognized them as the terrorists from the park.

Patrick looked at them with an expression she

recognized. He was pleased with himself and going to rub it in.

"You couldn't get her, but here she is," Patrick said.

"You're going to tell us you planned to have her show up?" the blond asked.

"No, but I know how to take advantage of a situation."

Carrie's stomach roiled. She was coping with her altered view of Patrick—and the stupidity of what she'd done. She'd trusted Patrick, and she'd been so desperate to get information about her father that she'd let him trick her into getting close, and now she was trapped.

"Where is my father?" she asked.

"Shut up," he snapped.

The blond young man leaned on his crutch and kept his gaze on Patrick. "This isn't working out the way it was supposed to. I'm shot in the leg. Bobby's still in custody, and he's not going free, is he?"

"It's not my fault that he got caught."

"This whole deal was your idea."

"Rita Madison's idea," Patrick corrected.

"How?" Carrie gasped out.

Patrick spared her a glance. "I said shut up."

"I trusted you."

"Oh, really? Is that why you sent me on that wild-goose chase into D.C. and hid in the pool shed?"

She could tell that really bothered him, and she

knew she'd better answer carefully. "I didn't want to do it, but Wyatt insisted."

"Blame him," Patrick snarled.

"Patrick, I thought you and I were friends."

"Oh, sure. On a limited basis. You and your father always thought you were better than me."

"No. Of course not."

All along she'd thought Patrick was on her side, but now she understood that their friendship was only an illusion. She saw the hatred on his face. Hatred that she wouldn't have believed if she hadn't seen it for herself.

Still, she couldn't stop herself from trying to reach him. "Don't you understand that Dad gave you every advantage?"

Patrick snorted. "Not like he gave you."

"I'm his daughter."

"And I was always just an afterthought. Or later, someone convenient he could use for jobs that needed getting done."

Seeing she wasn't going to get him to change his mind, she asked, "You hatched this whole plot?"

"No. It was Rita's idea. But I liked the way she thinks. Big."

"But why?"

"After the way her husband was pissing away money with his compulsive gambling, she needed some cash, and I knew where I could get it. She had the connections to pull off what looked like a terrorist attack—and to set you up."

Carrie gripped the arms of the chair where she sat, trying to anchor herself to reality when the whole world felt as if it was sliding out from under her. Everything she'd thought about the past few days was all wrong. "Are you saying it wasn't really a terrorist attack at all?"

"In a way, it was. An attack on you and your father, actually." He laughed. "Rita knew exactly how it would go once you ratted out the 'terrorists.' She knew you'd end up down at the Federal Building."

"But why set up an elaborate scheme?"

"Don't you know the insurance policy your father bought you pays triple if you're killed in a terrorist attack?"

"He bought me an insurance policy?"

He grinned. "Well, I did it for him. He was so out of it that he didn't even know."

She felt sick as she stared at him in disbelief, trying to rearrange years of thinking. Her father had done everything for this man, and it turned out that all he felt was resentment for not getting more. He'd hidden it well. She hadn't suspected a thing, but Wyatt had obviously had a very different view of her father's chief of staff. He hadn't trusted him from the beginning, and she should have listened to him.

Although bitterness had festered in Patrick for years, she wondered if he would have acted against her and her father without Rita.

But it was clear that he was enjoying crowing about his exploits, and she wanted to keep him talking, because the longer she stalled, the better chance Wyatt had to rescue her, and she had no doubt that he could do it.

"How did you meet Rita?" she managed to say.

"I was driving your father to a reception at her country club, and the old man let me come in and mingle with the guests. Rita and I hit it off right away."

"It was her idea to kidnap my father?"

"Yeah."

"Do you know where he is?"

"As a matter of fact, I do."

As they had gone back and forth in their revealing conversation, Patrick had taken his gaze off the blond man with the crutch. Now the blond pulled out a gun and pointed it at Patrick.

"Enough of this blathering."

Patrick stared at him in disbelief. "I'm in charge here."

"Not anymore." He punctuated the announcement by raising the gun and firing.

Carrie stared in disbelief as Patrick staggered back against the wall, blood spreading across his left shirtsleeve.

From his hiding place, Wyatt heard a gunshot. Then everything was quiet again.

Lord, had Patrick or someone else in the house shot Carrie? What was going on in there?

Rage boiled up inside Wyatt—rage and disregard

for his own safety. As one of the pursuers came close to the bramble thicket, Wyatt sprang out and grabbed the man, taking him totally by surprise and throwing him to the ground.

The gunman tried to twist around, tried to get his weapon into firing position, but Wyatt slammed his gun hand against a rock, and the man screamed.

"Eric?" the other guy shouted from what sounded like twenty-five yards away.

When Eric tried to answer, Wyatt slammed a fist into the man's face.

Blood leaked from his mouth, but he kept struggling. Wyatt pulled him up and slammed him against the ground, knocking the wind out of him.

He felt as though he had superhuman strength as he grappled with the guy, slamming him against the ground again and again until he went limp.

Wyatt picked up Eric's weapon, just as the other man came charging through the underbrush.

He saw Wyatt and fired.

A MUFFLED BLAST came from outside, then another. Two gunshots. Carrie's heart began to pound. When she started to spring out of the chair, one of the dark-haired men put a hand on her shoulder and pushed her down again.

"Stay put," he ordered.

"That's Eric or Cory taking care of your friend. What's his name? Wyatt?" the blond-haired man said.

"No," Carrie breathed. She *would not* believe that

Wyatt was dead. Not the Wyatt Hawk who had saved her and himself so many times since the attack at the Federal Building. These men had to be wrong. They couldn't see what was happening out there. They were just guessing, and if *she* had to guess, she'd say that it was the other way around. Wyatt had eliminated the threat from the other two men.

IN THE WOODS, the bullet missed Wyatt and hit Eric. Wyatt shot at the man charging forward, felling him with a slug to the chest. As he toppled over, Wyatt sprang up with Eric's gun in hand. When neither of the attackers moved, he knelt by each of them in turn, feeling for a pulse in the neck. There was none in either man.

He turned away from the two attackers he'd downed.

How many more were in the house, and was he in time to save Carrie?

With a gun in each hand, he ran toward the house through the woods. But when he reached the open area at the edge of the trees, he stopped.

At the moment he didn't give a damn what happened to himself, but he had to stay alive—to rescue Carrie. For so many reasons. But the one that came zinging into his mind was—he loved her.

The thought was so powerful, it nearly felled him.

He loved her? That conviction had slipped out without his conscious knowledge.

But as soon as he admitted it, he knew it was true.

He'd fought against it with all the emotional resolve he could muster. In spite of that, he'd fallen in love with her, and if he couldn't save her life, there was no point in saving his.

Stopping behind a tree trunk, he scanned the facade of the house. All the shades were drawn, and as far as he could tell, nobody was looking out. Still, instead of rushing right to the dwelling, he moved cautiously through the woods, circling around so that he could come at the house from another angle.

He had to succeed. He was Carrie's only hope.

Chapter Nineteen

Carrie looked in horror from the gunman to Patrick and back again.

Patrick's mouth began to work, and words slowly came out of his mouth. "Bruce, why did you do that?"

"This deal was supposed to be easy. She was supposed to die in the woods. Then it was going to be at the Federal Building. But the whole thing is turning to crap. Nothing's gone the way it should. I rounded up a whole crew of guys for you. And look what's happened. We lost George and Perry downtown. We lost Billy to the Feds. We lost Harry and Jordan at the safe house. I got shot there. And we haven't gotten more than a couple of thousand dollars out of this."

"You will," Patrick wheezed.

"The hell with your insurance-policy bull. I want you to grab that money you got out of the old man's account when he was drugged up and transfer it to us."

"That's *my* money," Patrick objected.

"Not anymore. I want it in a bank account where I can get my hands on it. And if you don't do that right now, you're dead. Or maybe I'll shoot you in the kneecap next time, then carry you to the computer so you can get that cash."

Patrick's face was ashen. "I need medical attention."

"You mean like I got after the safe house?"

"That's not my fault."

"Well, you just have a flesh wound. You'll live." The blond man looked at Carrie. "We may need you for a while."

"Want me to put her in with the old man?" one of the other terrorists asked.

"Come on, Sid—do you think it's smart to put them together where they can plot something sneaky?"

"I guess not."

"My father's *here*?" Carrie gasped.

Nobody bothered to answer her. The man who had pushed her down into the chair pulled her up and kept a tight hold on her arm as he escorted her out of the room. As she walked, she was processing information. Inez had said her father was acting demented. But it wasn't because his mind was deteriorating. It was because Patrick had been drugging him so he could get access to his financial resources.

The other man yanked Patrick up and led him to a computer on a table along the wall across from the front door.

The last she saw of him, he was wincing as he sat

down in the chair. No doubt he'd be transferring the money he'd stolen from her father's account, as the gunman had ordered.

As Sid led her down the hall, she looked at the closed doors. There were three bedrooms in the house, and her father must be in one of them— if these men were telling the truth.

She swallowed hard, then called out, "Dad?"

"Carrie?" her father shouted from behind the nearest door.

At the sound of his voice, she felt her heart stop then start to beat in double time. Her father really was here.

"No talking," Sid warned.

Unwilling to give up this opportunity, she ignored her captor and kept talking to her father. "Are you all right?"

The dark-haired man slapped her across the face so hard that her ears rang. "If you try that again, I'll shoot you," he growled as he dragged her farther down the hall.

In the far bedroom, he pulled out handcuffs and fastened her to the brass headboard.

"This mess is all your fault," he said bitingly.

"My fault? That's crazy. I was just minding my own business when I heard your plot."

"And now look what's happened."

The murderous look in his eyes told her he couldn't see the situation rationally. Better to shut up and try to figure out how to escape.

To her relief, he stomped out of the room, and she breathed out a little sigh. She was safe for the moment, but what about Wyatt?

Her throat clenched. "Wyatt," she whispered. "Oh, Lord, Wyatt, please be okay. What would I do without you now?"

The life she'd made for herself had been fine until she'd heard the terrorist plot in the park. Then it had turned upside down, and Wyatt Hawk had stepped in to right it again. At first she'd hated being forced into living with him. Then she'd come to realize that he gave her something she'd never had before. He wasn't just her bodyguard. He was a man who could be her partner—if he'd allow himself to think in those terms. But could he? And what had those shots outside meant?

She yanked on the cuff that held her to the bed. She had to find a way to free herself and her father. And then she had to find Wyatt.

A tall order, but she wasn't going to simply sit here and wait for the men out there to come back and kill her.

AT THE BACK of the house, Wyatt heard something that made his heart leap. Carrie called out to her father, and he answered. They were both alive, thank the Lord.

He listened to the sound of a door opening. Someone moved around before the door closed again.

The action was followed by profound silence.

Cautiously he crept toward the window. When he looked inside, he saw Carrie sitting on a bed, pulling at a pair of handcuffs that secured her left wrist to the bed.

After waiting for a moment to make sure that the guy who had cuffed her wasn't coming back, he tapped lightly on the window. She looked around, her eyes widening as she saw him.

Wyatt, she mouthed as she pressed her hand over her heart.

He felt a choking sensation. Putting his hands against the window glass, he pushed at the sash, but it was locked, and breaking the glass would bring the bad guys running.

When she saw what he was doing, she stood and tried to get to the window, but her cuffs kept her from getting close. After looking over her shoulder toward the door, she began to tug at the bed, moving it inch by inch closer to the window.

She would tug, then wait to make sure nobody had heard the legs scrape on the floor, then move it again, but apparently, the men were busy in the living room.

It took her several minutes to get close enough to the window to reach the lock. She unlatched the lock with her free hand, then pushed the window up. As soon as she opened the window a crack, Wyatt reached under and helped her shove it up.

Stepping back, she gave him room to climb

through the window, and he made it into the room and took her in his arms, holding tight.

"Thank God you're all right," they both said at once.

"I heard a shot," he said.

"One of the men shot Patrick. He was working with them. But it sounds like the crazy scheme was Rita's idea. If I had to guess, I'd say she had her husband killed by the guys out there."

He nodded, looking at the cuff that held her wrist to the bed.

Taking out a Swiss Army knife, he used one of the implements to manipulate the lock on the cuffs. When he heard the lock click, he pulled the cuff off of her.

She threw her arms around him again and held tight.

"How many men are here?" he asked.

"Three plus Patrick. A blond guy named Bruce who has a wounded leg—from the safe-house assault —and a couple of dark-haired men. One of them is Sid. I don't know the other one's name, but I saw him at the picnic area. I assume some of them were at the Federal Building."

"And I assume each of them is armed."

"Yes. But Patrick is out of commission. The one named Bruce shot him in the leg."

"Why?"

"I guess to make him understand that bad things

were going to happen if he didn't get my father's money out of the bank account where he'd stashed it."

Wyatt muttered a curse. "I guess this isn't going the way Patrick expected."

"Yes, and there's more. Apparently, Patrick was drugging my father—giving him something so he couldn't think straight. And so Patrick could have the run of his computer."

She gave him a pleading look. "My father did everything for Patrick. Why did he turn on him?"

"You said your father was...difficult. If *you* felt that way, how did a guy who wasn't a real member of the family feel?"

She nodded.

"We can talk later."

"Yes, my father's here. We have to free him."

"I heard you call to him. Where is he?"

"In the next bedroom."

"I guess we're going through the window again."

He helped her outside onto the ground, wishing he could make her get the hell out of there before the men inside discovered what was happening, but he knew from experience that she wasn't going to take orders unless she thought they made sense.

BACK IN THE great room, Bruce pushed himself up using his crutch.

He looked at his partners. "I expected Eric and Cory back here by now."

The other men nodded.

"You don't think that Wyatt guy could have gotten them, do you?" Larry, the third man, asked.

"They're good."

"Maybe he's better. And they should have taken the assault weapons. Get them out." He thought for a moment, then turned to Sid. "And maybe you should go back and get the prisoners. If anything's going to happen, we can use them as human shields."

"Right."

Sid started toward the back of the house.

WYATT AND CARRIE moved silently to the other window. Apparently, Douglas Mitchell had heard them, because he came over to the window and looked out cautiously. He was also wearing a cuff, but there was a length of yellow rope attached to it and the end was frayed.

He unlocked the window and pushed up the sash.

"I sawed through the rope," he said as he started to climb through the window.

He was halfway out when Wyatt and Carrie heard a shout behind him, then a blast from a gun.

Douglas made a startled sound, toppled through the window and landed hard on the ground.

Carrie bent to him.

"Dad? Dad?"

Wyatt leaped to the window and returned fire into the bedroom. Whoever was shooting inside ducked back into the hall. A moment later, footsteps pounded toward the great room.

Douglas pushed himself up, looking dazed. Wyatt saw a streak of red along the side of his head that disappeared into his hair. When he felt the track of the bullet, he found that it had traveled across the man's skull.

"It's a graze," Wyatt said as he helped the older man to his feet. "We can't stay here. Come on."

"Where?" Carrie asked.

"Out of the line of fire."

Carrie and Wyatt each took one of her father's arms, holding him up as they hurried him toward the woods.

They had almost reached the shelter of the trees when they heard shots behind them. This time it was automatic weapons firing.

They pulled her father into the woods. Blood dripped down the side of his face, and his skin was pale, but he was still on his feet.

When they were behind the trees, Wyatt spun around and returned fire. "You have to get your dad out of here," he said to Carrie, reaching into his pocket and handing her the car keys. "I'll hold them off. If I'm not there in ten minutes, take off without me."

When Carrie hesitated, he said it again. "Go. You have to get your father to safety."

He watched panic, fear, determination chase themselves across her face. He could see she didn't want to leave him, but she didn't want her father in danger, either.

"Have the engine running for a quick getaway. I'll follow you."

She reached for him, pulling him close. "I can't let you do this."

"You have to."

She clung to him for another moment, then took her father's arm and moved him farther into the woods.

Wyatt stayed behind the tree. The last time he'd been entrusted with a woman's life, he'd let her get killed. It wasn't going to happen again.

He studied the house. It was quiet. There were still three of the terrorists in there, all armed. The ones who'd come after him in the woods had been using automatic handguns. The ones in the house had switched to more powerful guns.

They'd use their superior firepower to rush him, and maybe he could stop them. But by then Carrie would be gone—if she followed orders.

CARRIE HELPED HER father through the woods, trying to hurry. When he stumbled, she held him upright.

"We can't leave Wyatt," she murmured as she helped him along.

"Agreed. But what are we going to do?"

"Are you all right?"

He laughed. "I'm a tough old bastard."

"You're not a bastard."

"Of course I am. I was always tough on you and Patrick. I've gotten worse. I can see that now."

"Don't blame yourself for this."

He scoffed, then was silent for several moments.

They made good progress through the woods. It was easier going than when she and Wyatt had approached the house. The downward slope helped, and they had already cleared some of the brush away as they came up.

Her father spoke again. "I made a big mistake."

"Dad…"

"Let me say this. I knew Patrick resented his place in our household. I tried to make him feel more like he belonged, but it was never going to work. I should have encouraged him to go out on his own. Instead, it was easier to let him take over some of my workload."

"You couldn't know what he'd do."

"I do now. He drugged me and started draining money from my accounts."

Did her father know that Patrick had also taken out a massive life-insurance policy on her? If he didn't, she wasn't going to mention that nasty detail.

As she helped her father through the woods, she racked her brain for a plan that would get Wyatt out of there.

He had told her to drive away. It was the right thing to do—for herself and for her father—but she couldn't leave Wyatt up there waiting for the men in the house to rush him.

The terrible image of that gun battle made her heart pound. He thought he was doing the right thing, but she wasn't going to let him sacrifice himself for her—not if she could do something about it. But what?

They made it to the car.

"Lie down in the backseat. I'll get you to the hospital as soon as I can," she said to her father.

"I'm all right. What are you planning?"

"I'm thinking," she answered, picturing the scene at the top of the drive. Wyatt was in the woods. There was a huge brush pile in the front yard next to Patrick's car. And beyond that a circle of blacktop at the end of the driveway.

Opening the glove compartment, she rummaged inside. When she found a box of matches, her hand closed around them.

"I've got an idea," she told her father. When she told him what it was, his breath caught, but he didn't try to talk her out of it.

She turned on the engine and checked the gas gauge. Plenty of fuel.

After cutting the engine, she climbed out and pulled off her slacks, then removed the cap from the gas tank. Using a stick, she stuffed one pant leg down into the tank. When she pulled it free, she saw it had acted like a wick, soaking up gasoline.

Next, she walked along the shoulder of the road for several yards and found a rock about the size of a baseball. Being careful not to touch the soaked part of the pant leg, she tied the rock into the garment. When she'd finished her preparations, she turned the car around and started up the driveway toward the house. The tricky part came next, but it seemed like her only option.

As the car came into view on the access road, the men inside the house started shooting, and she ducked low, clenching her hands on the wheel. But it seemed that Bruce, Sid and the other guy were too far away for accuracy. If they got her, it would be with a lucky shot.

Staying low, she pulled up on the far side of Patrick's car, using it and the brush pile for a shield as she climbed out.

Screened by the car and the heap of sticks and dried foliage, she lit a match and touched it to the end of the gas-soaked pant leg, rearing back as it flamed up with unexpected fury. As the heat leaped toward her, she heaved the garment toward the brush pile. The rock she'd tied inside the pants carried it forward, and it landed in a nest of dried vegetation and weathered wood that caught fire almost instantly.

Carrie crawled back the way she'd come, gravel digging into her hands and knees. As she climbed back into the car, a heavier volley of gunfire erupted from the terrorists, and she heard Wyatt returning fire from the woods, keeping the men in the house.

She waited with her heart pounding, willing the smoke to billow up enough for her to risk driving close enough for Wyatt to jump in.

It seemed to take forever, but finally she thought she had created enough of a smoke screen.

Ducking low, she took off, heading for the patch of woods where Wyatt had made his stand, and she saw him lean out from behind the tree and shoot toward the house, giving her cover.

When she drew close, he dashed through the smoke and leaped into the passenger seat. Even through the fire and smoke, shots followed her as she sped backward down the drive, then turned around and kept going. Some of the bullets hit the vehicle.

"Is everyone okay?" she shouted.

"Yes," her father and Wyatt both answered.

"I told you to get out of here," Wyatt growled.

"I wasn't going to leave you."

The gunfire faded behind Carrie as she sped down the drive. She had done it. They had gotten away.

Then her eyes widened as she reached the end of the access road, which was now blocked by a large black SUV.

Chapter Twenty

Men leaped from the SUV, and Carrie saw that they were wearing vests that said FBI. She also saw that they were aiming weapons at them.

"FBI! Come out with your hands up!" a tall man shouted.

"We'd better do it," Wyatt said between clenched teeth as he set his weapons down.

In the backseat, Douglas sat up.

As Carrie climbed out, she wished she was wearing more than a shirt and panties.

"I'm Wyatt Hawk and these are Carrie and Douglas Mitchell. Three of the armed terrorists are still up the hill in the house," Wyatt said as soon as he was out of the vehicle. "Patrick Harrison is also up there. They shot him."

While he was speaking, other agents circled around him and looked into the car. One of them reached under the dash and opened the trunk, then walked to the back of the vehicle.

"There's an assault weapon in here," he reported.

"Captured from the terrorists," Carrie answered.

She held her breath, then sighed in relief as the Federal agents conferred, then lowered their weapons.

"I'm Agent Fitzgerald," the man who'd been speaking said. "What's on fire up there?"

"I started a fire in a pile of brush in the driveway so I could get Wyatt out of there," Carrie answered as she lowered her hands.

Wyatt and her father did the same.

"How did you get here?" Wyatt asked.

"The maid, Inez, got your license number when you were at the estate," Fitzgerald answered. "You got away from the Mitchell house just as we arrived in the gardener's van."

"If that was you, who was shooting?"

"The terrorists had gotten there ahead of us. They took some shots at us, then got the hell out of there."

Carrie caught her breath. "And Inez is okay?"

"Yes." The man addressed Wyatt. "We had your make and model, but we didn't pick you up on a traffic camera until a half hour ago. We saw you'd altered the plates."

Carrie sucked in a breath. "Inez was helping you?"

"Yes. She was reluctant to work with us, but we persuaded her to cooperate. She put a tracker on your car." He gave Wyatt a wry look. "But you found it and got rid of it."

"I thought the bad guys had put it there," Wyatt said.

"Yeah, well, we weren't coordinating very well—

seeing as we didn't know whether you were part of the plot."

Carrie's voice rose in outrage. "Part of the plot? He's the only reason my father and I are alive."

"You gotta admit, your activities looked suspicious," Fitzgerald answered.

"Because we didn't know who we could trust. You do understand what's been going on?" she prodded. "Patrick Harrison and Rita Madison hatched a very elaborate scheme to kill me and get money from my father."

Fitzgerald nodded. "We're going to need more details from you. Like, for example, this started off looking like a terrorist plot against the government, but it appears to have been directed against the Mitchell family all along."

"Correct," Wyatt said.

"We'll tell you everything we know," Carrie said, then looked at Wyatt for confirmation.

He nodded. "It seems the men at the house were hired help."

Several agents peeled off and started up the driveway on foot. Above them came the sound of a helicopter.

"We'll get the rest of them," Fitzgerald said.

"You have Rita Madison?" Wyatt asked.

"We brought her in for questioning after intercepting a phone call she made to Harrison's cell phone. But that's not enough to arrest her. We have to prove that she's part of the conspiracy."

"Patrick claims it was her idea," Carrie said. "Maybe you can get them to rat out each other."

"Hopefully," Fitzgerald answered.

"And do you happen to have something I can wear?" Carrie asked.

One of the men went back to the SUV and brought her a pair of trousers. They were too long, but she rolled up the legs.

A siren told them another emergency vehicle was approaching. It turned out to be an ambulance.

Wyatt looked at Carrie. "You go with your father to the hospital."

"Where are you going?"

"I have to show them where to find the bodies in the woods."

She sucked in a sharp breath.

"Bodies in the woods?" Fitzgerald inquired.

"Yeah, two armed men came after me, and I defended myself." Wyatt looked at Fitzgerald. "Come on. I'll show you."

Carrie watched Wyatt and one of the agents disappear into the woods, wondering when she was going to see Wyatt again. Or *if* she was going to see him.

He'd saved her life. Now he had the perfect opportunity to disappear.

An FBI agent named Gleason followed the ambulance to the hospital. He stayed with Carrie while her father was treated.

"He needs to go home and rest," she told Agent

Gleason when her father joined them in the waiting room.

Gleason considered the request and turned to the elder Mitchell. "We can talk to you tomorrow."

"Thank you."

The agent looked at Carrie. "But I want you down at headquarters."

"Is Wyatt Hawk there?"

"Yes, but you can't see him now. We need to get your stories separately."

"To make sure we tell you the same thing?" she asked.

"It's the usual procedure."

She sighed, knowing there was no point in arguing. She ached to see Wyatt, but the sooner she got this over with, the better.

Her father spoke up. "Carrie, I'm sorry you had to go through all this."

"I'm fine. Thanks to Wyatt Hawk."

"We both owe him a lot."

"Yes."

"And there's a lot I want to apologize for. There's nothing like thinking you're going to die to make you realize what's important."

She swallowed hard. "I found that out, too."

They hugged, and she waited with him until a cab picked him up.

She spent the next three hours with the FBI, telling her story, confirming details and asking questions.

"Did Rita have her husband killed?" she asked.

"No, it was the mob. They wanted their money. It added up to more than forty thousand dollars. He'd stolen twenty thousand by forging his wife's name on a check, but it wasn't enough to pay them off. We assume he was planning to disappear."

"That's the twenty thousand dollars he had in his safe and noted in his little book?"

"What book?" Fitzgerald asked.

"Before he died, he gave us the combination to his safe, and Wyatt found the book and the money. We thought he'd gotten a payment for telling the terrorists when I was going to be at the Federal Building."

"Yeah, that would have made sense, only it was Rita who told them. She probably got the information from his computer."

"We followed her and saw her go to her bank. She looked angry when she came out."

"She must have found out that the money was missing."

The phone rang, and the agent picked it up. After listening for a few minutes, he swung back to Carrie. "Patrick is under guard in the hospital, and he's telling us everything he knows, trying to cut a deal."

"Good. Well, good that he's talking. I don't care what happens to him now."

They had more questions for her, but finally the session wound down, and she decided to take a bathroom break. On the way back, she stopped short when she saw Wyatt talking in the hall to one of the agents.

He looked up, spotted her and went very still.

She walked up to the two men and addressed the agent. "Mr. Hawk and I need to talk—privately."

"Of course." He pointed toward a nearby door.

She turned and walked toward the door, hoping she looked confident even though her chest was so tight that she could barely breathe.

For a moment, she thought Wyatt wasn't going to follow her, but he stepped inside a room that was furnished like a lounge with comfortable sofas and chairs and a couple of square table and chair sets.

Turning, she faced him.

"Were you going to leave without seeing me again?"

"That might have been the best thing."

"Why? Because you're a coward?"

Anger flared in his eyes. "Of course not!"

"But you thought it would be easier to just walk away from me."

"It would be better for you."

"Why?"

"Because I'm a former CIA operative who isn't fit for polite society."

Her anger jolted up. "Don't give me that old story. You think because your partner did something stupid in Greece, that you have to keep punishing yourself?"

When he didn't answer, she asked, "Do you love me?"

He went absolutely still.

"Are you afraid to tell me the truth?"

She saw him drag in a breath and let it out. "No. I love you," he said in a barely audible voice, then said it again more strongly.

She closed the distance between them, throwing herself into his arms, and he caught her, clung to her.

They held each other for long moments before she raised her head and he lowered his. Their lips met in a long, passionate kiss.

Carrie reached behind him and locked the door.

"What are you doing?"

"Making sure nobody can come in here," she answered as she reached for his belt buckle.

"This is the J. Edgar Hoover Building. You can't do that here."

"Watch me."

He swore under his breath, but he helped her free himself from his pants and helped her off with hers. They had been through hell together over the past few days, and she couldn't be subtle about the emotions churning through her. She needed him, and she needed him now. And it looked as though he felt the same desperation. He kicked his pants away and kicked a chair aside so that he could set her on one of the tables.

She spread her legs for him, guiding him to her, gasping as he entered her.

He went still immediately, his face strained.

"Carrie, did I hurt you?"

"No."

She sealed the reassurance with a hard kiss, her hands clasping his shoulders then moving down his back to his butt as he began to move inside.

They were both too emotionally charged for the lovemaking to last long. She felt her inner muscles contract, felt her whole body quicken as an all-consuming climax seized her. Moments later, he followed her into the maelstrom. They clung together for long moments before he eased away and picked up her borrowed pants, handing them to her.

"In case they send an assault team to break in, you know," he said as he found his own pants.

When they were both dressed again, he scooped her up in his arms and carried her to the sofa. Sitting down, he cradled her in his lap, and she nestled against him.

"Tell me you're not going away," she murmured.

The long silence made her stomach knot.

"Wyatt?"

"You really want me to stay?"

"Yes. I love you."

His breath caught. "You hardly know me."

"Maybe I don't know a lot about your background, but I know exactly who you are. You showed me over and over when we were on the run." She raised her head and looked at him. "You're the bravest man I've ever met."

"But—"

"No protests."

She pressed her fingers to his lips. "I'd never met

a man I wanted to spend my life with. I thought I'd always be alone, so I focused on my work. When I first met you, I thought you were another overbearing male."

"I was trying to keep my distance."

"I figured that out. And I appreciate it. But everything changed when you risked your life to save mine."

"I was doing my job."

"And more. So much more," she murmured, raising her head to kiss him again.

She knew they hadn't settled everything. But he wasn't going to walk away from her, and they had the time to work out the details. Maybe he'd even like the idea of coming with her on some photo shoots—to places she'd feel uncomfortable by herself.

She was going to ask him about that when a loud knock sounded at the door.

"You alive in there?" someone called out.

"Yes," Wyatt answered in a husky voice. "We were having a private debriefing."

She stifled a giggle.

"Oh, yeah. Well, the two of you are free to go—and find a room," the voice added. "But we'd like you to be available."

"We'll be at my apartment in D.C.," Carrie called out.

Footsteps departed.

"I hope they're not waiting outside when we open the door," she said.

"They're FBI agents. They're discreet."

She grinned at him, and he grinned back. She'd never seen Wyatt Hawk so relaxed, and she liked it. They needed more of that and every other good thing. Together. For the rest of their lives.

* * * * *

LARGER-PRINT BOOKS!
GET 2 FREE LARGER-PRINT NOVELS PLUS
2 FREE GIFTS!

⟨H⟩HARLEQUIN

super romance®

More Story...More Romance

LARGER-PRINT BOOKS!
GET 2 FREE LARGER-PRINT NOVELS PLUS
2 FREE GIFTS!

❧ HARLEQUIN®

Romance

From the Heart, For the Heart

HRLP13R

LARGER-PRINT BOOKS!

HARLEQUIN *Presents*

PASSION
GUARANTEED
SEDUCTION

GET 2 FREE LARGER-PRINT NOVELS PLUS 2 FREE GIFTS!

Reader Service.com

Manage your account online!

- Review your order history
- Manage your payments
- Update your address

---

*We've designed
the Harlequin® Reader Service
website just for you.*

Enjoy all the features!

- Reader excerpts from any series
- Respond to mailings and
  special monthly offers
- Discover new series available to you
- Browse the Bonus Bucks catalog
- Share your feedback

Visit us at:
ReaderService.com

RS13